THE BIG KISS-OFF OF 1944
by Andrew Bergman

"[Jack LeVine is] a reasonably self-respecting struggler in the Philip Marlowe tradition . . . LeVine is admittedly plumpish and bald, but not so sweaty that he can't exchange the odd meaningful glance with a classy dame. . . . The way Bergman manages to maintain both the spirit of affectionate parody and the impetus of his own story is remarkable and the early 1940s repartee is well up to standard." —*Times Literary Supplement*

Also available in Perennial Library
by Andrew Bergman:

HOLLYWOOD AND LEVINE

THE BIG KISS-OFF OF 1944

BY ANDREW BERGMAN

PERENNIAL LIBRARY
Harper & Row, Publishers
New York, Cambridge, Philadelphia, San Francisco
London, Mexico City, São Paulo, Sydney

First PERENNIAL LIBRARY edition published 1983.

Library of Congress Cataloging in Publication Data

Bergman, Andrew.
  The big kiss-off of 1944.

  (Perennial library ; P/673)
  Reprint. Originally published: New York : Holt, Rinehart, and Winston, 1974.
  I. Title.
PS3552.E7193B4 1983   813'.54   83-47579
ISBN 0-06-080673-7 (pbk.)

---

83 84 85 86 10 9 8 7 6 5 4 3 2 1

For Louise

IT WAS A THURSDAY MORNING and I had lots to do, like sip black coffee out of a cardboard container and stare out my window at the file clerks shuffling paper in the building across the street. I was starting to play with a molar when I heard my outer office door open and turned to see a blonde girl, maybe twenty-five years old, closing the door and taking a seat under the War Bonds poster.

"You can come right in," I called. "Most of the crowd has gone home."

She got up, straightened her skirt and walked in very quickly. She was tall and composed, with blue eyes that burned through too much face powder, a small mouth and a perfect nose, absolutely perfect.

"You're Jack LeVine?" She sat down across from me.

"I am so far."

"That's funny," she said. I didn't think she meant it and couldn't have cared less, not at 10:30 A.M. I cared more when she slowly crossed her legs and shifted in the chair. Bodies like hers didn't happen without work, except to a lucky few. I had seen a few of the few, usually a couple of hours into rigor mortis. Things were rough all over.

"I need what they call a shamus," she said.

"Is it Yom Kippur already?"

"Excuse me?"

"Forget it." I say a lot of dumb things before noon. "Why?"

"I hardly know where to begin, Mr. LeVine."

"Begin at the dirty part. It's been a slow week."

"Are you always this awful to people who want to engage

your services?" There was a little of the dowager in this, like a brushstroke of blue in the hair.

"Always. You'll like me a lot better when and if you get to know me. Everybody says so. Cigarette?"

She shook her head abruptly, distractedly, like someone who's nervous and wants to get on with it. Someone like her, for instance.

"Okay. Down to business. What's your name?"

"Kerry Lane. I'm a chorus girl." She looked instinctively at her legs. So did I. "I hope I'm out of the chorus, actually, and on to better things. Right now I've got a bit speaking part in *GI Canteen*." She looked at me questioningly.

"Don't look at me. I quit going after *Abie's Irish Rose* folded. It was my favorite."

"It was," she said tonelessly. "Anyhow, I play the kid sister of the lead's girl friend. The girl is Helen August?"

I knew who Helen August was but I shrugged like I didn't know, because that's the kind of guy I can be on Thursdays.

"It's not important. I come out when Helen and her boyfriend, Jerry Swanson, are necking. It's the night before he goes off to fight the Japs."

"Sounds like a real tension-breaker," I said.

She grimaced. "I get my laugh." She tilted her head like a teenager and stared at her nails. I was starting to warm up to Kerry Lane. "And it's a lot better than sitting in Schwab's Pharmacy for three years, waiting for Hollywood to get the idea."

"It didn't?"

"Not the vaguest. You might have seen me in a few crowd scenes and I once walked past Jimmy Cagney and Ann Sheridan in *City for Conquest*. It wasn't enough to keep me in chili. I decided that eating was better than starving and took a bus cross-country. It was a long ride. Now I'm working pretty regularly, eating, and living clean."

2

"And that's why you need a detective?"

She smiled for the first time. Not enough to light up the Polo Grounds, but pretty good all the same.

"It's not all that clean. I'm being blackmailed, by a man named Duke Fenton. Have you ever heard that name?"

"No." This time I wasn't lying. "What does he have on you?"

"I made a couple of films in California that I didn't tell you about." I think she might have blushed a little, but I wouldn't swear to it. "You might see them at your next Elks smoker. I was desperate for money, so anything they asked me to do in front of the camera, Mr. LeVine, I did." She paused. "You're shocked, I suppose."

"A little. Not enough to cause heart failure, but a little. Okay?"

She smiled a little smile. "Okay. Ordinarily, blackmail like that wouldn't count for much in New York. People here are just a teensy bit jaded."

"I've noticed. So what's the catch?"

She looked a little startled by the predictable question.

"Well, the catch is the producer of *GI Canteen*. His name is Warren Butler and he's a very important man, and also he's a straight-laced old fairy who'd throw me out of the show in a second if he found out about those films."

"Miss Lane, I seriously recommend that you go to the police with this."

She shook her head, very emphatically. "There's too much chance they'd come asking around the theater. I can't lose this job. I thought if you'd just see this man and . . ."

"Put the slug on him?" I finished her sentence, laughing. She was a card, this one was.

"Just let him know that it isn't worth all the trouble. He's barking up the wrong tree if he expects to make a great deal of money."

"Is it worth the trouble to me? A penny-ante chiseler can

get just as trigger-happy as a big timer. Maybe more so; he's got less to lose. I'd hate to die trying to rescue a couple of stag films."

She looked hurt and not very tough at all. Her hands were trembling.

"Please help me out." The voice was very small now. She took out her wallet and peeled off a twenty. And had a great deal of trouble separating it from the other fresh twenties. She noticed me gawking at the roll.

"Pay day."

"That's some bit part."

Kerry Lane stared at me, unblinking and afraid, like a deer who lifts his head from the grass only to find some schmuck in a red hat looking at him through a rifle sight. Her eyes went all wet and one tear cut a trail across her face powder. The skin beneath the mask was a lot softer and younger than I had figured on. She put the twenty on my desk and got up.

"Is that enough for now?"

I nodded. "I haven't done anything yet."

"He's staying at the Hotel Lava, the one with the steam-bath. It's on West 44th."

And she was out the door, leaving me to consider my black and encrusted window again, checking the file clerks. Twenty minutes before my mind had been as quiet and motionless as a hassock in an empty living room; now it felt like Macy's on the day before Christmas. I kind of liked it the other way, but Kerry Lane's story, plus those twenties you could cut your hand on, had me figuring angles on top of angles.

After sitting for a few minutes, spinning pipe-dream theories, I decided to go and find out the presumably boring truth. I took my green hat—the one with the red and blue feathers in the band—off the moose head I keep over the files, closed the office door, and locked the outer door. I rubbed a little grime off the frosted glass tl.at read "Jack LeVine, Private Investigator" and walked on down the hall. After I rang the elevator bell, the old cage took the Cape of Good Hope route before reaching nine.

Eddie, the snot-nosed elevator boy, ragged me.

"Another slow day, Mr. LeVine?"

I smiled and lit a Lucky, being careful to blow the smoke in his face.

"I took a real tomato up to nine before," he went on. "Looked kind of upset on the way down. Friend of yours?" He never turned around, but just kept talking to the gate while I talked to his black, greasy hair.

"My maiden aunt from Russia."

"Looked like a blackmail case to me. Main floor, Mr. Le-Vine. Have a pleasant day."

I bought a paper from Max in the lobby, just to look inconspicuous, although the way I figured the Lava, I wouldn't be noticed if I strolled in playing the maracas bare-assed.

My building, at Broadway and 51st Street, is a structure supported by the sheer density of the cigar smoke and cheap cologne fumes that rise from the agents and song pluggers who occupy most of its twenty-five stories. The Lava was eight blocks away, so I walked. And regretted it.

It was one of those sneaky days in mid-June when the temperature casually creeps up to about eighty-eight degrees and you're marooned inside a wool suit and long-sleeved shirt. After walking a couple of blocks, I took off my jacket and the wet circles under my arms were already the size of catchers' mitts. I felt terrific—a perfect day to track down a chiseler in a steambath. The eight blocks past hot dog joints, arcades, schlock jewelry stores, burlesques, and every other shakedown in the world was never the greatest walk in the world. Today it positively stank. In flusher times I would have taken a cab, but the last month's business—a couple of tail jobs and a joke bodyguard routine for a rich pansy who thought his ex-roommate was trying to kill him—put the nix on cabs for a couple of weeks.

By the time I got to the Lava, I couldn't have taken my shirt off without a pair of scissors. I perspire a lot—it's the kind of affliction you try to live with gracefully, like baldness another characteristic that makes LeVine unique among private dicks. Plenty of cops are skinheads, but most of the shamuses I've known had hairlines that started just a cut above the eyebrows. For me, baldness has become a trademark, a distinguishing trait: "Get me that bald dick, whatis-face, LeVine." People like a bald guy, like they like a fat guy

The Hotel Lava looked just like you'd think it would: a soot-covered ten-story building with a five-by-five marquee over two narrow glass doors with nobody to open them, and a neon sign that probably said: OTEL L VA at night. Inside it was worse, with a lot of dull gray chairs and a brown carpet that last got cleaned when Lucky Lindy had his big parade. The people matched the furniture: hookers, old men, and draft dodgers, sitting as quietly as if they were having their portraits done. In a thousand other lobbies in a hundred other cities sat the same people, with the same clothes, faces, and rackets. They put their cigarettes out on the same mud-brown carpets, read the same box scores, looked over the same kind of women and the same kind of men. In another half-hour, some of them would go to the track, one of the girls might turn her first trick of the day, or her tenth. It's a great life.

I walked over to the desk clerk, a shark-faced man with enough dandruff to fill a pillowcase and eyes that had seen everything and long since stopped caring. He was probably no more than forty years old.

"Is there a man named Duke Fenton staying here?" The shark turned and looked over the register, then turned back to me with total disinterest.

"Yes, there's a Mr. Carl Fenton registered."

"What room?"

I received a smile for my trouble.

"I'm sorry, hotel rules forbid me giving out that information."

6

"This dump hasn't had any rules since the Spanish–American War," I told him, and he started leafing through the *Daily News*. Nothing like a clerk fishing for a dollar smear at 11:30 in the morning to get the day off right.

"Sorry, sir."

I pushed a dollar across the desk.

"805."

"You're a credit to your profession," I said and walked off, already unhappy about the whole set-up. And even less happy when the elevator operator surveyed me with beady eyes the color of sewage. He easily weighed four hundred pounds and had a fan mounted directly next to his head which blew the sweat off him in sheets. Whoever was dumb enough to stand next to him got sprayed. I was dumb enough. It wasn't anything like walking on the beaches of Cape Cod. He stopped at five. The baths were on five.

"I got to pick up a package," he grunted. "Be right back." He kept the door open with a stop, so that the steam seeping out of the baths could fill up the elevator. The temperature must have been 105 and my shirt was a sponge. I could make out some pale, naked bodies moving around through the window on the door leading into the baths but the elevator jockey had somehow vanished into the gray mist.

Ten minutes later, as I was considering whether or not to pass out, he returned.

"Where's your package?" I asked.

He said nothing, but kicked out the stop and shot us up to eight. His uniform was soaked. I got out.

"Keep your nose clean, shamus," he croaked, closing the doors, "or I'll sit on your face."

A sweetheart. The place was filled with them. After the impromptu steambath on five, the eighth floor felt like a refrigerator car. A cleaning lady was airing out 801, letting in some fresh soot, and two doors down was 805. I'm not an investigator for nothing: show me 801 and I'll find 805 two times out of three.

I knocked on Duke Fenton's door and stared at my feet, waiting. No answer. I knocked again, a little harder, and drew another blank. When I tried the door, it was unlocked so I pushed it open with all due caution, my right hand tickling the Colt I keep in my jacket pocket. The room was yellow, small, and perfectly quiet. Some dirty white curtains were billowing inward ever so slightly. There was a suitcase propped open on a chair and a white shirt on the single bed. It was just back from the·laundry. Except for the pair of Florsheims sticking out of the bathroom, and except for the dead man inside them, everything was as it should have been. Forget the "excepts": the way this case was shaping up, everything was in order.

IT WAS A PRETTY JOB: two in the chest, one in the temple. I turned Mr. Mortis a little on his side and found his wallet. It was empty of cash but full of identification. Carl Fenton, Carl Fenton, Carl W. Fenton, and one card in the name of Fenton W. Carswell. Cute. So far I was definitely getting my twenty bucks' worth. I turned the late Fenton back to where I had found him and washed my hands, then crept over to the door and slipped the Do Not Disturb over the knob. I knew Fenton wasn't in any hurry to have his bed made, and it would take the cleaning lady a good long time to get that bathroom floor in shape.

Fenton's suitcase looked untouched. I opened the latches and went through his possessions. I carefully lifted his boxer shorts and undershirts, only to find more shorts and a couple of ties. I liked the one with the little cocktail glasses on it. He had two pink shirts, a black shirt, and a white shirt. Underneath a towel he had stolen from the Hotel Metro in Pittsburgh I discovered cologne, socks, and an unopened box of condoms. Poor bastard: it told the whole story of his stay in the big city. Almost the whole story; that hole in his head added a nice touch.

My search of Fenton's effects kept me occupied, but I hadn't found anything useful and I had the nagging feeling that I wasn't about to. The room was as spare as a monk's, with its one dresser, one closet, single bed, and two-by-four throw rug. Hunting through it was as easy as it was futile. Satisfied that the law wasn't going to find Kerry Lane's Oscar-winning performances, I picked up the telephone.

"Yes?" It was the shark at the main desk.

"Get me the police."

There was a silence you could have driven two Packards through.

"Perhaps the house detective may be of assistance."

"Okay, sure. Tell the house dick that there's a man wearing three bullet holes who's modeling them on the bathroom floor in room 805 and he's been holding his breath for a long, long time. It's a hot day, so if your man wants to figure out what happened, he better do it fast or else the smell is going to put a real crimp in your afternoon business. Johns are nervous enough without dead guys checking in and out. The cleaning lady is in 804 right about now; if you want, I'll ask her to dispose of the body. Unless, of course, you'd prefer me to throw it directly out the window and claim suicide. The *Mirror* will love it: 'MAN SHOOTS HIMSELF THROUGH CHEST AND HEAD, LEAPS FROM HOTEL LAVA.' Or maybe, in a pinch, you'll connect me with the police."

"You being funny, mac, or what?" I was now addressing the house detective.

"Come up to 805, the laugh's on me." I hung up, walked over to the door, and removed the Do Not Disturb. The cleaning lady was backing out of 804 across the hall, pulling a wagon loaded with gray sheets and cleansers. She turned and saw me.

"Morning," she said in an accent that surprised me: Cockney. "You with the party in 805?"

"No, and you'd better stay out of 805 for a while. There's been a little accident."

She peered in. With the door open, there was a cross breeze that had the curtains floating almost horizontally across the little room. She saw the black shoes sticking out of the bathroom.

"Oh, dear," she said, with no more emotion than if she had just dropped a can of Dutch Cleanser. Probably less. "Is he dead, then?" I nodded and she just shook her head. "I'd better go into 806 and clean up there, don't you think, until this gets cleared up?" I agreed and she pulled her wagon to 806.

"He didn't look too nice," the cleaning lady said, opening 806. "That one in 805. Looked like a bad sort."

"Did you notice any visitors here?" She just looked at me. Something in her brain had flashed COP and I had lost my chance to have a little chat.

"No, no. Nobody," and she was inside 806.

I heard the elevator doors open down the hall, so I went back into 805, sat down on the room's only chair and lit up a Lucky. The shark-faced clerk and a large moon-faced man in dark, billowing slacks, a white shirt, red vest and a black, clip-on bow tie came into the room. Without knocking.

"You're under arrest," said the shark.

The house dick laughed and I felt a lot better. At least somebody was sane in this hotel. The dick had a brown crew-cut and a nose the size of a pear. His eyes were friendly and cynical.

"Don't get your shit in an uproar, Mel." He looked at me and past me, to the Florsheims resting at their forty-five-degree angles. "Call the cops, Mel."

"There isn't anything? . . ."

"Call 'em, for Crissakes!" Mel, the shark, left in a huff.

The house dick shook his head. "Don't mind Mel. He's just an asshole." It was a final-sounding statement. All the credits and debits had been counted up and the verdict was in: Mel was an asshole. The house dick went into the bathroom and looked over the body, while I let the cigarette smoke skate through my lungs and out my nose. I heard the water running, and the dick came out of the john, with the bored and sardonic look of a man who had worked in cheap hotels much too long.

"A professional piece of work," he said. "No fuss, no muss."

"Maybe he was doped up. Doesn't look like any struggle at all."

He gave me a long, humorous look. His eyes were very blue and surprisingly clear, but the pallor and crow's feet were of a man who had spent his life being baked by fluorescent lights. "You a shamus?"

"I'm Jack LeVine," I said, like it meant something, and handed him my card. He read it over and stuck out his hand: "Toots Fellman," and I shook that hand. He was the first decent guy I'd met that day, maybe the first one in a couple of days. You can go a long time without . . .

"You had business with this creep?" he asked.

"I never got the chance to find out. I knocked on the door a couple of minutes ago and there he was, smiling at me."

"You get to know a little in this racket. When that son of a bitch registered, I knew he wasn't in town to sell cole slaw. I told Mel I'd keep an eye on him." He sat heavily on the bed and looked toward the bathroom. "Guess you'd say I did a helluva job." Toots laughed and unclipped his bow tie.

I just shrugged. "You notice anything about the mug while he was in one piece? Anything out of the ordinary?"

"Not a thing. He played it close to the chest. Maybe people were up here, maybe they weren't. I couldn't sit outside his room and he sure as hell didn't do business in the lobby. He was a pro, a guy who faded into the woodwork."

"A pro killed by a pro," I said. "Except for the stiff, this room looks set for afternoon tea."

"Think he got sapped before he was shot?" Toots asked.

"If he didn't, he must have fainted."

Toots went back to the bathroom and checked out what was left of Fenton's head. "On the money, LeVine," came the voice from the john. "Evidence of swelling back here. He might have gotten it falling on the floor, but I'd bet you're right." I heard the water running again. It was a messy job, looking at Duke Fenton. Toots came out wiping his hands on his pants.

"So far, I'd say there was some double-crossing in the air," he said.

"You might be right," I told him casually. He was eventually going to want to know what I was doing here. Eventually was now; Toots eyed me, more quizzically than suspiciously, and finally asked, "Can you tell me why you were here?"

"Nope. Nothing major, though, nothing that would end up in a stiff. He was shaking down somebody, but the stakes weren't big enough for anything like this. Besides, she's too delicate to have slugged somebody and then shot him three times, with three bull's-eyes."

Toots raised his bushy eyebrows. "You free-lance dicks get all the good ones."

"Just in the movies, Toots. I figure Fenton was shaking someone else down, more likely a couple of people, and somewhere along the line, it made sense to put him on ice. But my case is small potatoes."

Toots smiled and then said something very nice: "You want to get out of here before the law shows up?"

"It'd save me a lot of useless lying. Might even save me a punch in the mouth."

"I'll call Mel and tell him to let you out. You can do me a favor sometime."

I stood up and shook Toots's hand. I felt like marrying the guy. "Come over to my office sometime soon, Toots. I'll buy you a drink out of my closet."

He was already at the phone, calling the desk. "It's a deal," he said, winking at me and patting me on the shoulder as I breezed out the door. The smell was starting to get a little thick. "Mel," I heard him say as I started down the hall, "let the shamus out. He's all right. Because I fuckin' say so, that's why."

The elephant who ran the elevator was waiting for me down the hall. When I walked into the elevator, he stepped far aside, like I was carrying the plague, and I stood in the back, to avoid the saltwater douse.

"You think you can find your way down without another steam break, slim?"

"Why don't you chew on this, shamus?" He pointed to one of his four hundred pounds, somewhere vaguely around the middle of his body.

"Sorry, I like my meat lean."

"Funny man," he said out of the side of his mouth, turning his head a little. He spoke with a kind of dignity: a rhino coping with a gnat.

"Just observant," I told him. The elevator stopped in the lobby and I got out, stroking fatso on the head, "Nice boy."

"I'll see you again, wiseass."

Mel wasn't too happy to see me walk out the door without getting worked over. He gave me his best shark smile.

"Thanks for everything," I shouted over to him. "I'll tell my friends to stay here when they're in town." I pushed my way out of one door just as three husky cops and a couple of detectives, one of whom, Paul Shea, I knew all too well, pushed their way in the other. Like ships in the night. Shea didn't see me, but it was very close, too close. Another minute spent insulting a fleabag desk clerk and Shea would have had me sitting on the hardest chair in his office for a couple of hours. I would have told him I was at the Lava for the baths and he would have sipped some more coffee and asked me again what I was doing there. That's how those things go.

Out on the street again, I took a deep breath. The air was rank and heavy, but it smelled a lot better than the dead man in 805. Going back to the office meant having to speak with Kerry Lane, and I wasn't ready for it, so I told myself I was hungry and walked over to a good sandwich and coffee joint on West 47th Street, to kill time and read the first edition of *The Sun*.

I took an end stool, which gives you the most counter-space, and spread out my paper. I ordered a tuna on toast, light on the mayo, and found that *The Sun* was pretty happy: our boys were making their post-D-Day rounds of Northern France and the locals seemed to like them a lot better than the Nazis. Everybody was saying it would all be over within a year. Governor Dewey was making noises about the need for new blood in the White House. I remembered him well from the days when he ran the D.A.'s office, when the cops I knew were saying he'd sell his grandma to make page one in the afternoon. President. That was a laugh. A goddamn ambulance chaser.

I really wanted to soak up the box scores, to follow the exploits of wartime baseball's one-armed outfielders, and blind, deaf and dumb infielders, but I was trying to figure how I had wandered into a murder in the space of less than two hours. World wars were all very interesting, but the stiff in 805 had me staring into my coffee long before I could drink it. The feeling was unmistakable. I have it on one case a year, maybe every year and a half: I was getting in over my head. Every time I opened a door, someone would topple over with footprints on his face. And then there was Kerry Lane. She was going to call me and ask how it went; I'd tell her Fenton was dead and she'd gasp and I'd try and figure out whether or not she'd been rehearsing that gasp in front of a mirror for the past couple of hours. And if she had known he was dead, why make a sucker out of me for the alibi? But I believed her at 10:30, and if I believed her then—with Fenton already giving the bathroom floor a paint job—I ought to believe her now. So I read the box scores. The St. Louis Browns had shut the Yankees out and Stuffy Stirnweiss went 0 for 4. What was the world coming to, anyway? And what did I care about Stuffy Stirnweiss, who would be off the team when the real Yankees returned from Europe and the Pacific?

A counter woman whose hair was just a little too black for the lines around her eyes smiled at me.

"More coffee?" I don't look half-bad when I keep my hat on.

"No thanks." I took a stab at gallantry. "What can I do for you?"

"Well, for starters you could make this war end a little

15

faster. I got two kids over there, with Patton."

I managed some class: "Well, I'm sure they'll be home very soon," and felt very, very proud of myself. I left an extra dime under the coffee cup, folded my paper and got up.

"Mister," she said and smiled, smiled beautifully, "you left two dimes by mistake."

"No mistake."

"It's a mistake." She took the other dime and slid it toward me. "You didn't start the war and you didn't try to pick me up. Good luck to you." That was two good people in one day. I was pretty sure it couldn't last much longer.

It couldn't. I barely had time to close the office door behind me and throw my hat on the moose head—always a ringer—when the telephone started jumping around my desk. I wasn't prepared for the voice on the other end.

"Jack LeVine," came a husky female voice.

"Yes."

"Hold on please."

I held. I was connected.

"I'm speaking to Jack LeVine?" asked a man. His voice was a lot less husky than the girl's had been. I wished she had hung on a little longer.

"You are. Now let me play. I'm speaking to——?"

He laughed, a tinkling laugh like Chinese bells swaying in the breeze outside a cerise bedroom with lots of mirrors, a zebra rug, and the most divine four-poster bed.

"God, but you're an amusing guy. I'm Warren Butler, the producer."

"I'm honored. What can I do for you, Mr. Butler?"

"I'm afraid that I'd rather not discuss it over the telephone."

"Well, that's fine by me. How about leaning out your window and shouting it over?"

He laughed and laughed, and laughed. "I can see why

you're famous for your sense of humor, Mr. LeVine." I'm also famous for my black shoes, the ones with the black laces. This was beginning to smell like a herring taking a sunbath, just a little.

"Shall we play this game a little while longer, Mr. Butler, or can I just assume that you called me for a reason?"

"Quite right, LeVine." The putz was still chuckling. "I'd like to speak with you about a rather personal matter and was hoping we could get together as early as this afternoon."

"Let me check my book." I looked out the window. The air shaft was getting a little darker; maybe it would rain. "Looks good, Mr. Butler. What's the address?"

"You know the Schubert Building?"

"Sure. That's 45th Street."

"Right. I'm in 1107."

"That's a lucky number."

"It's stood me in good stead, Jack." I was "Jack" already.

"I hope it continues to. Things can happen in New York." He was silent for a few seconds. When he spoke again, his voice was deeper, less theatrical. I liked it a lot better that way.

"Three o'clock."

"That's jake with me," I said, and hung up.

I pulled a Blatz out of the little half-icebox which building regulations forbade me from owning and/or operating. But no law of man or nature would stop me from having an ice-cold beer every afternoon of my adult life. Snow or sun, wet or dry, the brew helped me think when I needed to think, helped me nap when I needed to nap. It helped me remember and helped me forget. You probably get the point.

This particular afternoon required a little thought. A lot of questions were reaching me at once, and none of the answers. Did Butler want to talk about Kerry Lane's blackmailing and, if so, how had he found out? Did he want to talk about Kerry Lane, but not about blackmail? If that was the case, what was the connection with her and did it mean she was holding things back from me? Did Butler's call have nothing to do with Kerry Lane, just a fabulous coincidence that might earn me a place in Ripley's "Believe It Or Not"? And it didn't even stop there. If Butler knew about the blackmailing, what did he want from me? If he needed a cover-up, he had a half-dozen press agents to do the job, all of them willing to toss themselves under the Twentieth Century Limited to keep Butler's name free of taint.

Or was I simply about to get used?

My phone rang again and it was Kerry Lane, breathless with panic. Or playing someone who was breathless with panic.

"Oh, Mr. LeVine, are you all right?"

"I've got a little gas. Otherwise, I'm okay."

"I was afraid you were hurt."

"Not like your friend Fenton. He's not much fun to be with."

"He was murdered?"

"You sound like you know plenty. Tell me about it."

"Please, Mr. LeVine, don't be so cynical. I walked past the Lava about an hour ago, God knows why, but I felt I just had to go by and look in. There were squad cars and an ambulance. I stood around like a tourist and finally got the nerve to ask some cop what was going on. I was so afraid that you'd been hurt, Mr. LeVine, that my knees were knocking."

I said nothing, but just listened and tried somehow to decide whether or not Kerry Lane was telling the truth or reading from a script. Until I was sure, I couldn't afford to tell her about Butler's call. She was either the kind of girl who might panic and take that long step out the window, or the kind of girl who played her emotions like a poker hand. One way she'd get hurt, the other way I'd get hurt. Or get dead. So bringing up Butler couldn't do anybody any good, not right now. I decided to play both sides until I knew what the hell was really going on.

"After I asked the policeman," Kerry went on, "he just smiled and said 'a slight case of homicide, honey, nothing catching.' He thought the whole thing was a joke."

"You get a funny sense of humor working homicide. It happens after you see too many people with hatchets and ice picks sticking out of their heads."

"Please, Mr. LeVine, I still feel nauseous. The cop didn't tell me who'd been killed and I didn't want to look too curious, so I ran for a phone to make sure you were okay. I'm in a pay booth."

"Kerry, did Fenton ever mention anybody else in connection with his operation? Did you ever meet anyone else, a partner?"

"No one. I met him once, in that hotel, and there was no one around, no phone calls. It just seemed like a one-man operation."

"If that's true, you should be in pretty good shape with him out of the way."

"Maybe." She paused. I tried to make out what I could from that pause, but came up empty. I covered the mouthpiece and belched. I sometimes do that, if there's a lady on the other end. Cover the mouthpiece. "Mr. LeVine, did you find the films in his room? Please don't look at them."

"I wouldn't, if I had them, but I don't. I looked all over the room, which wasn't too hard, but all I could find was underwear and socks. There's two possibilities. One, he stashed his goods somewhere else—maybe in a Grand Central locker, maybe in his home base, if he had one, maybe with his mother. If that's the case, and he was working alone, you're home free. If he had a partner and that partner decided he didn't want to be partners anymore—which is always an angle in blackmail homicides—then we really haven't gotten anywhere. You'll be hearing from the guy."

Kerry Lane's voice got a little quavery. "But that would implicate him. We could blackmail him right back."

"Maybe, but not necessarily. He could say he had them

all along. He could say he bought them from a go-between. And we have no evidence. Plus, it would mean precisely the kind of publicity you don't want if we even tried to blow the whistle on the mug."

She was crying now, and all I could do was look at my moose head. The operator asked for another nickel.

"Mr. LeVine, I've got to get out of this."

"Listen, Miss Lane, we can get out of this if I have some inkling of what I'm doing. You are quite sure that you have told me everything I ought to know? If not, I'm going to hang up and get a hold of some more life insurance. This isn't a simple little blackmail case anymore, not when stiffs start getting into the act."

She pulled herself together, a little too quickly to suit me. "I don't think you need to know any more, Mr. LeVine. You have sufficient information." My ear was getting frost-bitten. I was getting mad.

"Sufficient? That's a horse laugh, sweetheart. You're being blackmailed for a couple of stag films and that's it, except that the guy who's blackmailing you is suddenly a dead guy. Maybe it doesn't have anything to do with you, maybe we just wandered into something like innocent bystanders, but if you're holding out on me, toots, the odds are I'm going to wind up as the window display at Frank E. Campbell's."

"I'll call you later, Mr. LeVine. My nickels are running out and this isn't getting either of us any place." The click at her end sent a breeze through my skull. This was a great case for twenty bucks, any way you figured it. I was going through it with a tin cup and a cane and that's not the way I like to operate. Like it or not, it's not unusual. People hire a dick to do dirty work, like they pay a colored girl to clean up the john. The don't leave loose change around the girl and they don't trust a shamus to buy them the city edition. What they tell him is what they want him to know, which is never what he needs to know. But put two drinks in most people and they'll tell a private dick things they wouldn't tell their husbands or wives, life stories with nothing left out. Just like they'll confess everything to the cleaning lady while finishing off some afternoon sherry. And they do it for the same reason: neither of us counts. We do a job and disappear. I nursed that thought over my beer, staring out of the window. Maybe I'd ask Warren Butler if he wanted me to clean his john. My head wasn't in such pretty shape, but this racket still seemed a lot better than the dentist's life my mother had hoped for, or the fur business my old man had gotten stuck in. I couldn't kick, could I? The hell I couldn't. I finished the beer and decided to call Toots Fellman at the Lava.

"Hi, Jack. It was pretty dull."

"They didn't come up with anything?"

"They didn't come up with anything and it looks like they don't much care if they ever do. Shea was here. You know the guy?"

"We once had a little tête-à-tête under a two-hundred-watt bulb."

"Must've been pleasant. He's a pretty tough boy. Came up here, looked at the stiff, just kind of scanned the room and said 'inside job.' He's pretty sure a partner was involved."

"He knows Fenton was a shakedown artist?"

"Fenton had a record you could drive on from here to St. Louis. I got the distinct impression nobody's in much of a hurry to catch the killer, except maybe to pin a medal on him. Unless, of course, there's an angle nobody knows about."

"Not that I know of."

"Sure, you don't know a thing."

"Toots, you'd be surprised how little I know."

"Jack, I'm your friend. You forget fast."

"Maybe I'll know more tomorrow or the next day, but right now I'm sleepwalking and that's a fact."

"Give me half an hour, maybe I'll believe you. You welshing on that drink already?"

"You can pick it up early next week. Cleaned and pressed."

"No starch," he said. "If I hear anything else, I'll let you know."

At ten minutes past three, I picked my hat off the moose and sailed out the door. As always, Eddie took his goddamn sweet time cranking the elevator up to nine.

"Afternoon, Mr. LeVine. *Post* says there was a murder over at the Lava."

"Glad to hear it."

"You're a hard case, Mr. LeVine. Guess you have to be, in your business. When you going to show me the ropes?"

"Soon as you turn thirteen."

"I'm nineteen."

"Then what the hell are you doing over here?"

"Ah, don't be a heel, Mr. LeVine. I'm sole support of my old lady. I'd go over if I could. Main floor."

"Eddie, I'm a heel."

"You're really okay, Mr. LeVine, just a little cranky. I ain't all bad neither. Just show me the ropes someday."

When I hit the street, the air weighed a ton and everything that normally smelled bad on Broadway smelled a lot worse now. I'm a man of simple pleasures and all I wanted to do was play with the ducks in my bathtub and listen to a ball game. But I was too smart for that. I was going to play footsie with some mean pansy of a producer.

LOBBIES IN THE WEST FORTIES can be classified in two ways:
either they have a watery-eyed guy in khaki who sits on a
chair and wouldn't look up if you arrived in a tank, or there's
someone in a uniform who's nice enough but won't let you
move a step unless he knows where you're going. The man in
the Schubert Building wanted to know where I was going.
It made sense. The lobby reeked of prosperity. The black
floor was spotless, the walls were light brown marble, and the
lighting fixtures shot soft beams toward the ceiling, muting
everything. But you could still read a paper while waiting
for somebody. It wasn't a bad place to hang out.

Neither was Warren Butler's office—if you were Louis
the Fourteenth. The carpeting was deep enough to hide in,
and that went double for the receptionist, a redhead with the
kind of skin that made you think of Victorian heroines. A little
eye makeup and that was it: the rest was natural cream. Her
hair was piled up and you had the feeling that when it got let
down you were in for a very good time. Elegant behind the
desk and a tigress between the sheets. She made me nervous.

"You're probably Mr. LeVine." The voice sounded even
huskier than it had over the phone.

"Probably."

She smiled, politely. "Won't you have a seat?" I sat down
and took a good look around. It was the kind of outer office
that made you think hard about what you would say when you
got to the inner office. Subtly lit and smelling of cash, with
oil paintings of swells in red riding suits hung on dark oak
walls. You could get a good night's sleep in any of the chairs,
which were set about twenty feet from the receptionist's
desk. I looked over at the table next to me: it was so highly
polished I could have shaved by it. It might have been an

English club room, except that English club rooms don't have *Variety* and the *Hollywood Reporter* lying all over the place. If Butler wanted you to think he was the king of show biz, he did a hell of a job. I lit a Lucky and smiled at the redhead; she smiled at the Lucky. I had taken off my hat. A door opened in back of her.

"Jack, how good to see you." Warren Butler was a vision of loveliness, with a Miami tan and gray hair. His blue pinstriped suit looked like it had been made with him standing in it, as minions from Brooks Brothers swarmed about. His diamond tie-clip matched his diamond cufflinks. I wondered if he was going to lift his trouser leg and show me a diamond anklet. He had a large, bold nose, but it went well with big, piercing blue eyes, thick white eyebrows, full mouth, and a very tough jaw. Looking him in the eye was a lot harder than talking to him on the phone. Despite the snowy hair, he didn't look much over fifty. I figured him for a son of a bitch right off the bat.

Butler put his arm around my shoulder and guided me into the inner sanctum, turning to say, "Absolutely no calls, Eileen. I don't care if it's the White House." It was all so goddamn stagey that I expected his office to have footlights and an audience applauding my entrance. When I was through the door, I saw that there wasn't an audience, but not for lack of space. You could have run the Kentucky Derby in Warren Butler's office. It was forty feet from the door to his desk, forty feet of deep carpet, pool-table green, some couches the Yankees could have fit on comfortably, chairs in leather of deep burgundy, some colored jockeys holding ash trays, and the same King Arthur oak walls.

Lining those walls were rows and rows of photographs: Butler and Hepburn embracing, Butler giving roses to Katharine Cornell, Butler mock squaring-off with John Barrymore and toasting Noel Coward, Butler and Winchell in back of a microphone, Butler getting kissed by Carole Lombard. And I always liked Carole Lombard. Some other shots were of historical interest: Butler and Jim Farley chatting on some dais, Herbert Lehman whispering in Butler's ear, and one which I strolled over to with my hands behind my back: "To Warren, Thanks for a grand evening's entertainment. You're spoiling me terribly! Affectionately, Franklin Roosevelt." I was not playing in the minor leagues.

"I heard Mussolini used to have an office like this, before his show folded."

"Oh, no, mine is much larger," Butler said pleasantly, almost absently, as if he had thought it all out long ago. He directed me to one of those burgundy chairs, a mere six feet from his—practically spitting distance. It was a rich man's chair. Most people in this miserable world will die without ever sitting in something so firm and so soft, so supportive and so yielding. And there was a whole class of people who wouldn't know what a bench felt like, whose whole lives were upholstered, who took absolute comfort at all moments completely for granted. The chair felt so good I almost got a little sick. It served Butler well, this chair; it made you conscious of the ease and power with which he moved through life.

He was reading my thoughts.

"You know I wasn't born rich, Jack."

"Oh, no?" I said in no tone of voice at all. Like a sheep going "baa."

"Far from it. My father was a Polish mineworker from Scranton. My real family name would take you a week to pronounce." He smiled very carefully. "Dad came home at night and washed his face for half an hour before you could see that he was a white man. He went down to those mines every day but Sunday and after twenty years you could have mined coal out of his lungs. One night my old man came home and started coughing and didn't stop until he was dead. Forty-six years old."

"And that's when you turned to Communism." I felt sorry enough for his old man, whether the story was true or not, but Butler's life history was so rehearsed and polished that I felt like a Sunday feature writer for the Allentown *Picayune*. I don't like to feel that way.

"No," said Bulter, "that's when I decided that I couldn't stay in Scranton and have my own life mined away from me." I didn't doubt that he caught the edge of my remark; he just didn't care. The story rolled on, a rotogravure special: Warren Butler, Broadway's Mr. Lucky.

"I came to New York thirty-five years ago and gravitated to the theater right away. It had a kind of excitement then that I fear has long since faded, a kind of feeling between audience and performer. Jesus, those were grand days." He leaned back and lit a cigarette with long fingers. Butler was the kind of guy who blew the smoke toward the ceiling. "I swept up the Academy of Music when 14th Street was class in this town. I ran errands and got my nails dirty and finally got a job working for Flo Ziegfeld in 1916. He promised to hold my job until after the war. I went to Europe and the heaviest action I saw was in some French bedrooms." He laughed a "between us boys" laugh about as confidentially as if he were on the CBS radio network. I didn't say anything.

"When I came back, Ziegfeld made me his right-hand man. That was 1919; I was twenty-five years old."

"And the rest, like they say, is history."

"You're a cynical bastard, Jack," Butler said evenly.

I leaned forward, pulling my pants legs down a bit.

"Mr. Butler, the fact is you called me up to your office on a matter you said couldn't be discussed over the telephone. It's a hot day, a very hot day, and I walked here. Imagine my surprise when the big secret turns out to be your life story."

When he smiled, the temperature in the room dropped about forty degrees. Maybe he didn't like me anymore.

"You want to get straight to business, Jack, that's fine with me. I just thought a detective would profit by knowing something of his client's background. If that doesn't interest you, we'll move on."

"Your background interests me plenty, Mr. Butler, but

clients have a very human tendency to tell that part of their history which they want the world to know about. It's the parts they leave out that a private dick can use. Also, you're not my client yet as far as I know."

Butler stared at me bleakly and rubbed his cigarette out in an ashtray lifted from the Stork Club. It was the only human touch in the joint, except for the redhead outside. He then reached into a desk drawer and pulled out a sheet of paper.

"We'll now discuss what I didn't want to speak of over the phone. I'm sure you'll understand why, Jack. I believe that a young girl performer in my show *GI Canteen* is being blackmailed, or, rather, I'm being blackmailed because of her. She might be getting shaken down as well. That I don't know. What I do know is that I want it stopped. I want this man bought off or whatever one ordinarily does to chase away blackmailers."

"This is your first experience with extortion?" I asked, all innocence.

"Obviously," and now the temperature in the room was sufficient for the storage of meat. He definitely didn't like me.

"So any way I can get the guy off your back is fine with you."

Butler smiled. "Short of killing the man, I suppose. I don't want this to get out of hand."

"Mr. Butler, I've never had any dealings with you before. You're a sophisticated man, you must have dealt with detectives before. Why did you call me?"

He didn't look mystified, just bored and a little restless, like he wasn't used to having five-minute appointments run five minutes too long. "Oh, I don't know. I haven't had to deal with detectives, 'sophisticated' as I might appear. I asked one of my assistants to look up some respectable private eye in the phone book. He came up with you. Maybe it wasn't that simple, maybe he asked around, maybe he knew somebody who had employed you in the past and been satisfied with your work. Whatever he did, he came into my office this morning and put your name on the desk. Period. That's why I have assistants."

"I always wondered how I got hired."

"Now you know," Butler said, and his smile was the sunshine of the Arctic. "I received this note yesterday."

He handed over the sheet he had pulled out of his top drawer. It was written in the scrawly, five-year-old, untraceable hand of people who make a living out of hate mail, dirty mail and blackmail. I read:

Dear Mr. Butler:

You think "GI Canteen" is a patriotic show. I got some films made by one of your actresses a couple of years ago in L.A. They're not so patriotic, although sailors might like them. It'll cost you ten G's to keep me from leaking the story and to get the negatives and prints. Come to 14 Edgefield Road, Smithtown, Long Island, and we'll talk business. Friday, noon.

Friend of the Arts

"The handwriting is like a kindergarten reject, but that's a blind," I told Butler, handing back the letter. "This is a very sharp note, written by a pro."

"Yes," said Butler, smiling a little, "and not without a sense of humor. 'Friend of the Arts,' that's really rather funny." He stared down at the piece of paper. "Yes, he's obviously no amateur and that's why I have to have a pro on my side, Jack. If I attempted to handle this myself, I'd be in way over my head. If I went to the police, there's too great a danger of the whole town finding out."

That one I couldn't figure out. "A guy in your position, Mr. Butler? Just give out a lot of theater tickets and you could buy a couple of captains in Vice. They'd keep it so quiet you could hear money being folded."

"Perhaps, and perhaps I'll eventually take that chance, but for now I'd like to try and clear it up absolutely privately. The money isn't any big problem. I just don't want a mess."

"Either do I, Mr. Butler. These things can get very sticky." I didn't like this at all. Two shakedown artists, one already dead, the other waiting out on Long Island.

"I'll try and make it worth your while." Butler got up and walked over to a photograph of him with his arms flung around George and Ira Gershwin. I squinted and was able to make out an inscription which started off: "To 'Lucky' Butler," when Lucky pulled at the picture and it swung open on hinges. Behind it was a small wall safe which Butler opened with a few quick turns. He must have gone to it a lot.

"The Gershwins wrote 'I've Got Plenty of Nothin',' didn't they, Mr. Butler?"

"I believe so," he said, dry as dust. He closed the safe and pushed the photograph back on the wall. He was holding a wad of one-hundred-dollar bills.

"Do you think two hundred can hold you?" Butler said, thumping back in his chair. I got the feeling he was getting very bored with me and my jokes, just as I was getting interested. Very interested.

"I'll take a hundred for now. I get nervous when my bank account starts getting respectable. I might get soft and indolent, spend all my time taking a Pullman to Palm Beach or Jersey City or something."

"You've got a hell of a chip on your shoulder, Jack. This money didn't come easy."

I looked around the office, just for effect. "It must have been hell. By the way, I'd like to see *GI Canteen* this evening. Can you spare two tickets?"

"Doing research?" Butler smiled.

"Something like that." I got up, holding my hat. "I figure one of the girls will take off her clothes, just out of habit, and then I've got a big clue. You're sure you don't know which one she is?"

Butler looked at me very hard and I was a little afraid. For all his goddamned airs, he was a very hard man. "You're a real son of a bitch, Jack. The genuine article." He pushed a button on his intercom. "Eileen, give Mr. LeVine two tickets to *Canteen* for tonight."

"Fine, Mr. Butler," crooned the redhead. I was looking forward to taking a look at her again.

Butler stood up. "Jack, I don't like you one bit, but I don't have to. All I want is honesty and I'm sure I'll get that. Please come back here after you've been out to Smithtown tomorrow. I'll be here until seven. Hope you like the show."

On cue, his office door opened and Eileen was there with two long orange tickets, holding the door for my exit. I waved to Butler, "Warren sweetheart, you won't be disappointed. I'll be the greatest Hamlet you ever saw," and went to the outer office. It suddenly looked small.

"You wanted two for tonight?" Eileen asked, her left hand fussing with the back of her neck.

"Yes, but I get vertigo in the balcony."

"Then these shouldn't give you any trouble." She handed them to me, half-amused and half-bored by my little joke. She'd never heard of the balcony. The ducats were row C, center. I didn't get that close at St. Nick's on Monday nights, and ringside was only two and a half bucks, not five.

"I hope the girls don't sweat too much." The redhead's reply was to look at a spot above and beyond my right shoulder. When you're nobody, you're nobody, and no one has to laugh at your half-assed jokes. So I put on my hat and went out the door and down the elevator and out of the Schubert Building into the late-afternoon heat, a shmendrick getting paid by big people to do ugly work. I felt invisible. I felt like a six-foot, two-hundred-pound nothing. But I also felt like a nothing who knew a little something: that no matter how much he insulted Warren Butler, he had the job. That was pretty interesting. At least I thought so.

I WENT BACK TO MY OFFICE, took the phone off its hook, put my new C-note in the wall safe, replaced the phone and left to take the elevated out to Sunnyside, Queens, where I live. I can't afford Manhattan—can't afford the rents or the noise or the sadness on most faces. So after fifteen, twenty minutes of straphanging on the Flushing "L," where I lean against the vestibule doors and watch the backyards and factories and the easy flow of traffic and people, I'm home. People water their lawns in Sunnyside and the vegetable man says, "Jack, you're a schmuck if you don't buy the little tomatoes today," so I live there. Also, I've got a four-room apartment which sets me back thirty-eight fifty a month and neighbors who play poker and come in to listen to the ball games and the fights. And I used to have a wife, until she decided she'd be better off married to someone who came home three nights out of five and had an even chance of making it past fifty. It was as amicable as those things can be and now she's married to a sweet little guy in children's ready-to-wear who's home five nights out of five, at six sharp. We have lunch sometimes. My father and mother were upset but not shocked—with their only son doing such un-haimisheh work as being a detective. They would not be surprised if I turned Hindu and walked around New York wearing a white sheet.

The apartment smelled stale and close when I walked in. I opened a few windows and talked the cranky old Westinghouse fan into doing me a favor and turning around for a while. Then I called a gal named Kitty Seymour, who used to be a crime reporter and now did public relations for the fire department, and who liked me.

"Kitty, you want to see *GI Canteen* tonight?"

"Since when do you go to the theater?"

"Since producers give me free tickets."

"A producer who hired you to tail the leading lady?"

"Close, but no cigar. A producer who's being black-mailed."

"For what?"

"Do you know that's the third question in three sentences? It's a girl in his show who made some stag films once. He does family shows and doesn't want it to get around. Doesn't make much sense if you think too hard about it."

"I'd think he'd just fire her."

"He doesn't know who it is."

"But he's willing to pay for the films?"

"Ten grand worth."

Kitty whistled.

"Very strange case you've got there, Jack. Doesn't sound nice at all."

"It doesn't sound, taste, *or* smell nice, Kitty. But the guy's paying me in real money, a lot of it, so I'm pretending it's on the up-and-up."

"I'd get out of it."

"And you have an income. Listen, meet me in front of the Booth Theater at a quarter past eight."

"No dinner?"

"Post-theater snack, dear. The best people are doing it."

She laughed, a fine, full, honest laugh that made me feel good all over.

"The best and the cheapest. Eight-fifteen, Booth. Thanks, Jack. I'll be there, no questions."

She gave me a little kiss over the phone and hung up. I went to the kitchen and opened up a Blatz when the phone got lonesome and started ringing. I ambled into the living room and got it on the fourth ring.

"Yeah?" I said.

"Mr. LeVine, this is Kerry Lane again. I hate to call you at home, but I felt I had to apologize for my outburst this afternoon. It was childish and I'm deeply sorry for it. I should realize that you are in a difficult position."

"Well, right now I've got my feet up and there's a cold bottle of beer in my hand. That's not such a bad position, for openers. If you're talking about the case, I have something of a lead that's taking me out to Smithtown, Long Island, tomorrow. That ring any bells?"

"None. How did this come about?"

"I've been contacted by Fenton's playmate."

"He didn't waste very much time." She wasn't dumb, this girl, not dumb at all.

"Not a hell of a lot, no." I stared past my feet out the window. Some kids were shooting craps on the roof of the apartment building across the street. I wouldn't have minded playing with them for a while, even if the oldest was fourteen. Come to think of it, I wouldn't have minded being fourteen.

"Do you think there are more of them?"

"Well, if you've told me everything I ought to know, it stands to reason that this punk will be the last in the chain. Supposing that he and Fenton were in business together and Fenton crossed him and got croaked for his trouble, the partner figuring nobody would mind very much, the partner takes the firm's assets and makes it into a one-man business and that's the whole story."

"You're probably right." She sounded unconvinced. I waited for her to say something else. She didn't.

"Miss Lane, if you have nothing more to say, I'm going to hang up, not because I don't like chatting with you but because I have a beer to finish and a nap to take. Anything else?"

"No." She sounded as distant as someone calling from the Ukraine.

"Have a stiff drink and put it out of your mind," I told her. "In a day or two, the whole business will be wrapped up tight."

"Perhaps. Good-bye, Mr. LeVine, and thank you."

I hung up and discovered that something small and hard, something like fear, had found a comfortable spot in my stomach. Kerry Lane sounded terribly frightened, about something I was sure I knew nothing about. Maybe more than her budding career was on the line. Like her life. Like my life.

One of the kids shooting craps looked to have rolled up about thirty-five cents so far. He was doing better than LeVine, who stripped down to his powder blue shorts and curled up on the couch. You'll like the dream I-had: having just finished a performance of some kind, I am sitting in front of a dressing-room mirror, the kind that's ringed with forty-watt bulbs, rubbing cold cream on my face. Butler walks in with Roosevelt, Stalin, and Pete Gray, who had one arm and played outfield for the St. Louis Browns. He was the guy who would catch the ball in his glove, pop it up in the air while whipping off his glove, catch it in his bare hand and throw it back to the infield. Butler says, "Gentlemen, Jack here is a consummate performer," and then points a gun at my head, which is when I woke up. I thought maybe I'd try and figure it out, using my best City College Introduction to Psychology, but decided against it. I had better things to do, like open a can of Spam, fry an egg over it, and call it supper.

GI Canteen reminded me of why I never went to the theater anymore. Chorus boys prancing around in army outfits until I felt like puking; a number called "That's How We Do It in the U.S.A." in which a girl with tremendous knockers spilling out of her red, white, and blue bathing suit shot down a couple of guys made up to look like Hitler and Tojo, except that they looked like the butcher and the laundryman. Kerry Lane was so pale, even through the makeup, that Kitty nudged me the minute she walked on stage. Five years as a crime reporter does wonders for the intuition. After eating at Sardi's we went back to her place on East 68th Street.

Kitty's apartment was a spacious one-bedroom affair with plants and vases and good taste radiating from every corner.

She took my coat and asked if I'd care for some cognac. I said yes and went to the most comfortable-looking chair in the joint, where I lit a Lucky and thought about being in the apartment with Kitty. We'd had a funny kind of friendship over the past six months, a couple of divorced people making with the jokes and never really getting down to business. We had bedded down once, to nobody's particular satisfaction. I was a little drunk and had pretended to be even drunker.

Kitty came over with the cognac in a snifter and sat on my lap.

"How tired are you, Jack?"

"Very."

"I see." She smiled and put her hand in my lap. Kitty's rust-brown hair was piled high on her head and her green eyes shone with intelligence. "I had a wonderful time tonight, Jack. We seem to think very much alike." She wasn't making a pitch, just leveling. She emphasized her words by rubbing her hand, rolled into a small, loose fist, across my lap.

"I don't think I'm that tired."

She laughed. "I hate coy men, Jack." Her hand continued its intent but unhurried dance around my body. The ride got bumpy.

"How sweet," she said. Her hand stopped and flattened out against my fly. "No drunk act this time, Jack."

"Absolutely not. You may ravish me at will."

We stood up and headed for her bedroom, young and foolish, the private eye and his bimbo. Just like in the books.

In the sack we made that sweetest of discoveries: that we really *were* friends, great and royal and generous friends. That stuff you don't get in the books.

IT'S A GOOD TWO and a half hours out to Smithtown from Sunnyside, a terrible two and a half hours actually. I was tired to begin with and the ride in my aging Buick almost put me away: a vista of swampy lots, marshes, gas stations, and clumps of houses that looked like they didn't know what they were doing on Long Island when they could be in Brooklyn or Queens. I rubbed so many mosquitoes and gnats out on my windshield that it began to look like an aerial view of a battle-field. After forty minutes of squinting through their little squashed bodies to see the road, I pulled into a dusty red-and-white Esso station. The grease monkey, a thin man in green overalls, was sitting on a stool outside the office, drinking a Nehi. He got up slowly and walked over to my car.

The monkey was wearing a little green cap with the name "Bert" sewn across the front in yellow thread. He had the comic-sad green eyes of a man who hasn't had very much to laugh about, but has retained his sense of humor all the same. His nose was long and sharp and his teeth stained brown from years of chewing tobacco. I could see that Bert had stayed out in the sun too much: his skin had the texture of an old saddle. He leaned into the car and took a long look at my graveyard of a windshield.

"Bugs are just a bitch right now." His voice was thin and sounded like it wasn't used very often. Couldn't be all that much business ten miles east of Mineola, with nothing but weeds and telephone poles for company. "Heat or damp must have brought them out, way I see it."

"I think you're right," I told him, getting out of the Buick for a stretch. It was eleven o'clock and the sun was high and strong in the sky. By noon, everything would look shimmery.

I took a deep breath and the air felt heavy and syrupy. I coughed.

"Hot enough for you?" asked Bert. "Jee-*sus*, ain't this been a honey of a June for you. This damp is what's bringing out all the bugs." Including the one who had just gone from soup to mints on the back of my neck. I could feel the stinging and swelling already. This was going to be one hell of a day.

"Hey, Bert, you know your way around Smithtown?"

"I might, with my specs on." He had the car door open and was leaning across the front seat, spraying the windshield and rubbing the bugs off with paper toweling, then spraying again to towel off the last traces of blood.

"How about a street called Edgefield Road?"

"I know it." Bert climbed out of the car and went to work on the front of the windshield. "You're still a good forty or so miles away, but when you hit Smithtown, go right through what they call the business district—which means just a couple more stores than usual—and go another half-mile till you pass a joint called Cookie's Bar and Grill. If you got a minute, stop in and tell Cookie, Bert Little says hello. If not, keep going and you'll hit a street called Salem. Take a left and follow it all the way to Edgefield."

"You know it pretty well."

"Born and raised there, as they say. That Edgefield section is pretty well run down now. Nothing too fancy. You just visiting?"

"That's right."

"Well, there's better places to go. How 'bout some gas?"

I got out my ration book and filled the tank.

There were a lot better places to go. One hour later, drenched with sweat, feeling the dull ache of a possible cold and glowing with bug bites and sunstroke, I pulled up to Edgefield Road and parked on Salem, to grab a quick look-see. I turned off my motor, which was the only sound for miles, got out of the car and leaned against the door, reaching into my shirt pocket for a Lucky. It didn't take much of a look to realize that Bert was right: Edgefield Road was nothing too fancy.

Both sides of the street were lined with white clapboard bungalow-style houses, probably no more than ten years old but already decrepit beyond repair. Shingles were cracking, drainpipes were rusting and breaking off, and the paint was peeling off in wild, jagged patterns, leaving dark outlines against the sides of the houses that resembled the body-shaped holes made by silent comedians when they ran through walls. The hinges on half of the screen doors were busted, so doors flapped open and shut whenever the wind changed its mind. A couple of houses had small flower beds out front; most were surrounded by dirt, crabgrass, and every kind of scrawny weed that thrived and multiplied in the gases and exhalations of poor people. Broken earthenware pots sat marooned on the porches, next to chipped garden chairs, fallen hammocks, dreaming dogs, and all the quilts and rain-ruined blankets that get dumped in a corner and are never moved again. A couple of children were playing with the ground. There were no trees to protect them from the sun. I felt as distant from Manhattan as if I were tailing someone across the Sahara.

A wiry, thin-lipped woman with what you might call brown hair came out of number twelve Edgefield and saw me leaning against my car. She stopped and folded her arms across her white blouse. A little boy was pulling at her dull and baggy gray slacks, but she ignored him and stared at me. The kid was about four, dirty, pale, and barefoot in blue shorts and a tee shirt. I decided to make my move over to number fourteen and walked toward it, nodding pleasantly at the lady.

"Afternoon."

"Afternoon," she echoed back, without too much emotion one way or the other. "If you're going to number fourteen there, save your breath. Party living there left yesterday afternoon."

There wasn't any sign of life at fourteen and the driveway was empty. I stopped.

"Nobody home since yesterday?"

"That's right, mister." She looked about thirty and sounded closer to fifty, with a tired, uneven voice. Her eyes were gray and close together, separated by a good pert nose which was smudged with dirt. Her lips were thin and she gave off the look of a high school sweetie who had hit her peak at about sixteen and had been losing her looks, feature by feature, ever since.

"I was supposed to meet somebody there at noon today."

"Well," she said, shrugging her shoulders and pointing her head toward the house, "you're out of luck."

"It's important that I find the party."

"You a cop?" She was wary but not hostile. Not yet.

"Private cop."

Surprisingly enough, she smiled, a kind of close-mouthed, vulnerable smile. It was the spontaneous but tentative grin of a poor woman talking to a stranger, delighted about something but restrained by the fears that come from a lifetime of dependence on the whims of people with money.

"Like on the radio?" She looked down at her kid, who was gawking at the big bald stranger talking to his mother. "Paulie, this man's a private eye, like Boston Blackie." The kid kept staring at me, his arms hugging his mother's left leg.

"Boston Blackie gets paid a lot more than I do."

She laughed. "Yes, well he probably does at that." She looked around. "I couldn't tell you much about the people over at fourteen cause there was hardly anyone over there too much. I used to see two men walking around there occasionally. Sometimes they'd stay a few days, or a week. They looked a little rough, so I didn't speak with them a whole lot and told Paulie not to bother with them. On Monday and Tuesday of this week, there was one of them there, but he left yesterday afternoon. Looked like he was leaving for a while."

"How so, suitcases?"

"Only one suitcase that I could see, but he had some cartons that he was putting in the trunk of the car, which was a

39

black Ford sedan. You want to know the car, I suppose, the way Boston Blackie always does. That's always the first thing he asks about." She smiled shyly, delicately.

"It is helpful. Anything else?"

"Like I said, he had these cartons in the trunk and I had the feeling he wasn't coming back for a while, or somebody was after him or something, cause he really tore out of here." She looked down. "Remember how fast the man in the car was going, Paulie?" The boy nodded and turned away, putting one hand in his mouth and keeping the other bunched around the folds of her slacks. From the way she spoke to him, I got the idea she didn't have too many other people to talk to. She read my thoughts.

"My husband Earl is in the navy right now. Out in the Pacific Ocean."

I nodded respectfully. "Well, he'll be back pretty soon."

"That'll be great, won't it, Paulie, when Daddy's home?" She mussed the kid's hair and he hid his face in her thigh. "Paulie's shy with strangers."

"He's a nice boy. Would you mind telling me your name?"

"You going to call me to the witness stand?" She smiled again and I knew I was a big event in her life.

"Nope." I smiled as nicely as I could. I was out of practice in dealing with real people.

"Well, then I'm Mrs. Earl Rogers," and proud of it.

"Mrs. Rogers, if I broke into that house, would you be very upset?"

She kind of squinted at me. The wind picked up and we both turned our backs to it to avoid the dust. "Well sir," she said, "I can't see anything with this dust in my eyes, so I couldn't tell whether you broke in or not." The wind let up and we faced each other. I handed her five bucks.

"That's very kind of you," said Mrs. Earl Rogers, holding the bill very tight in her hand. "I appreciate it." There were no histrionics and no hint that she wouldn't accept it. "It'll come in real handy these days."

"You earned it."

"Guess I did." What she was thinking at that moment I'll never know. Maybe nothing.

"You got a personal card?" she asked. "In case something comes up." I handed her a card and she stared down at it. "Jack LeVine. Maybe you'll be on the radio someday." She put the card in her back pocket and stood silent for a moment, stroking the five like it was a baby chick. Then Mrs. Rogers turned and started walking back into her house. The kid was still staring at me, wondering who the hell I was. I couldn't have told him.

"You come in here, Paulie. Leave the man alone."

I watched the kid follow her into the house, turning around every other step to look at me. Then they were both inside. It was very hot. I undid the top button of my shirt and walked over to number fourteen Edgefield.

The driveway was empty except for a couple of beer bottles, gravel, and stray bits of tape and cardboard. I walked up three peeling white wooden steps and tried the door. Breaking in was going to be very easy because the door was ajar already. It required a push. I pushed and walked into a living room that had been cleared out in a big hurry. The linoleum floor was a garden of boxes, rope, wire, and tape, and the walls were bare except for a few pin-ups torn out of some sunbathing magazines and pasted up with their edges still ragged. Every hideout looks the same and, with one difference, this set-up fit the pattern. The same pulp magazines stashed in the corners, the same little metallic tables with stamped floral designs, the same beer bottles on those tables and, as always, cigarette butts floating in the beer. There was a couch covered in red corduroy and liberally sprinkled with ashes, playing cards—two jacks, a queen, and the six of hearts—some dirty argyle socks and a topping of crushed peanut shells.

Like I said there was a difference: the newspapers. Dozens of them covered the floor and the two chairs, swamped a glass-topped coffee table and ringed a torn-up black hassock. And these weren't just the New York dailies. "Friend of the Arts" had them from Philly, Newark, and Boston, even a couple of Washington *Stars* were scattered beneath the couch. And these papers had obviously been read; their edges were bent back and dulled, their folds flattened out.

But going through the papers didn't tell me a thing. The guy hadn't paid much attention to the sports sections, so the bookie angle was out, not that I gave it any weight anyhow. It was the hard-news pages that were most smudged and pored over. I picked through them, looking for marginal notations or whatever, but I could have been reading tea leaves for all I learned.

Being a dutiful if not inspired dick, I searched the house, knowing full well that I wouldn't find the films. Those cartons Mrs. Rogers had seen her neighbor carry out weren't filled with linen and silver service, that was for goddamn sure. But I looked anyway. I swept the peanut shells from the couch cover and its corduroy folds yielded the empty foils of a condom. At least the guy had some company. There were Clark bar wrappers in the fireplace and also a ball of paper which turned out to be an envelope addressed to someone named Al Rubine. The name didn't mean a thing to me.

My search of the "master" bedroom, a twelve-by-eighteen box which had once been painted coral, uncovered nothing. There was a rocking chair with a torn undershirt draped across one of its arms. When I touched the arm, it fell right off. An empty condom box—my respect for this guy was steadily increasing—lay under the bed. I opened the closet and found a half-dozen empty wire hangers. Then I went into the kitchen.

On the kitchen floor I found Governor Thomas E. Dewey.

He was neatly clipped and trimmed, and I found him shaking hands with a banker named Eli W. Savage. The newspaper photo was resting under a chair leg and it struck me as the second interesting discovery of the afternoon, the first being "Friend of the Arts'" no show. I couldn't tell what newspaper it was from, although Philly seemed a good enough bet. There was a fat caption which read: "New York Governor Thomas E. Dewey was greeted at the Philadelphia Bankers Association dinner last night by Quaker National Bank prexy Eli W. Savage, chairman of the association. Savage is being mentioned as a contender for a spot in Dewey's Cabinet, should the Republican hopeful go to the White House. The governor stressed the invaluable contribution the banking community has made to the war effort." Amen. If they stopped bothering me about my bum checks, they could all be canonized as saints. Bastards.

I sat down on a kitchen chair and looked the clipping over carefully, checking both sides to see if there were any markings or notes. There weren't. On the back of the clipping was half an advertisement for a sporting goods store—"Tennis Racket Bazaar"—but I somehow didn't think that tennis was the clue. It was this picture of Dewey and a banker and it didn't make a hell of a lot of sense any way you figured it. Except maybe one way, and that meant somebody was playing a very high-stakes blackmail game, maybe with a banker, big enough to pull him away from a ten-grand date with Warren Butler. It didn't seem like a very satisfactory way for this case to stand right now, but as long as the somebody had his Kerry Lane film stashed away in those cartons of shakedown bait, he could always call us again, on a rainy day.

There was a phone in the kitchen. I picked it up and was delighted to find it was still connected, so I dialed the operator and got her to connect me with Warren Butler's office.

"Warren Butler Productions," came eight syllables of careful modulation. Sitting in this Smithtown dump, I felt like I was calling Hollywood.

"Eileen, fire of my loins, tell Mr. Butler that Jack LeVine is on the line."

"Oh yes, Mr. LeVine. Mr. Butler told me that if you

called, I should ask you to come directly to his office. He doesn't wish to discuss any aspect of this matter over the telephone."

"Tell him if he doesn't come to the phone, he'll never see me in that office again. This isn't the goddamn movies."

"You don't have to berate me, Mr. LeVine. I merely told you what Mr. Butler's request was." Eileen sounded a little hurt. Just a little.

"I'm not blaming you, dear. Just put him on."

There was a pause, while I hung suspended in the limbo of "hold," on the borderline between communication and extinction. I listened to a dull kind of hum. As long as it was on "Friend of the Arts'" tab, I could wait for a while.

Butler sounded agitated when he broke into the hum. "Jack, for Christ's sake, I don't want to handle any of this over the phone."

"The cameras aren't rolling yet, Mr. Butler, so calm down. Stop acting like it's high espionage."

"This case may be a joke to you, Mr. LeVine, but I don't like being hounded by blackmailers. I think it's damned serious."

"Al Rubine doesn't think it's all that serious."

"Who the hell is Al Rubine?"

"He just might be the 'Friend of the Arts' we all know and love. Also, he's taken a powder."

I was back on hold and after Butler's hysterics, I kind of preferred it. The phone hummed to me a little more and when Butler came back about a half-minute later, he was a little more subdued.

"Sorry, Jack. Eileen came in with a telegram and I had to put you off for a bit. Now, exactly what is the story? I've had a madhouse of a day, so you'll have to excuse my snappishness."

"Don't worry, you're always aces in my book, Mr. Butler. The story is this: I showed up in Smithtown, which is a hell of place to be even if it isn't ninety-five degrees, a little after twelve o'clock. Number fourteen Edgefield looked deserted so I had a little chat with a lady who lives at number twelve."

"What's her name?"

"It's not important. She told me she used to see two pretty unpleasant-looking mugs hanging around number fourteen on an irregular basis. The house doesn't look too lived in, so it seems to check out. On Monday and Tuesday of this week, there was just one of them around. He came back last night, loaded up his car with cartons, took one suitcase and blew. The lady says he was driving very fast. The house is empty, except for a lot of boxes and newspapers lying around."

"Did you recover the films?"

"I said the house was empty."

"Jack, I've got to run," Butler said abruptly. "If you can be here by around six, I'll pay you the rest of your fee. See you then." The man was a whiz at getting off the phone. Having nothing better to do, I hung up on my end.

THE DRIVE BACK to New York wasn't all that interesting: weeds, gas tanks, and sun-baked concrete. I suffer in the heat and it was well over ninety. I also suffer from ignorance and what I didn't know about this case was enough to fill up a library wall. If "Friend of the Arts" was leaving this line alone because he had a bigger sucker caught on the other, there wasn't much to do but wait. Maybe not even that. Kerry and Butler might just say the hell with it and go to the police, but that was a long shot. I could be a sweet guy and tell Kerry that the producer knew someone in his show was being shaken down, yet I had a feeling that that wouldn't change anything.

Maybe the case was just beginning.

I reached home by a little after four, giving me time enough to stand in a cold shower, knock off some Blatz and a salami sandwich, and lie down to stare at the ceiling and ponder nothing more profound than getting in a good Friday night of poker. It didn't take a long time to figure out my needs. I was a basic model 1944 prole. Given plenty of beer and cigarettes, a sympathetic woman, the Yankees on a winning streak and poker at the end of my week, LeVine could be made happy. A simple man. I was very content working straights and full houses in my brain; when I realized that I had to go see Butler again at six, it was like awaking to discover that I had wet the bed.

Halfway into dressing, I heard the phone ring and hopped into the living room with my pants around my knees, like a guy in a potato race. I was pretty sure that Kerry Lane would be at the other end and wasn't disappointed.

"Mr. LeVine, am I disturbing you?"

"No, I was just hopping around the house."

"I see." She didn't know how to take it, so she didn't take it all. "You sound jovial. I hope that's a good sign."

"It's not a good sign or a bad sign, Miss Lane. When I got to Smithtown, there was nobody home. Fenton's pal had taken off the night before."

"With the films, of course?"

"With all kinds of things. This guy plays in the big leagues and I have a strong feeling that you and me are pretty small potatoes to him."

"Perhaps. Did you get his name?"

"Maybe. You ever hear the name Al Rubine?"

"No." There was a longish pause, so I held the phone with my neck and took the opportunity to pull my pants on.

"Do you think we should just tell the police?"

"Tell them what?"

"Well . . . that Fenton had a partner who probably killed him, and that the man is on the loose and dangerous."

"Miss Lane, a blackmailer knows fifty people with perfectly good and honorable reasons for killing him. Fenton probably shared that house in Smithtown with a partner. Once Fenton was killed, it made sense for his partner to get out with the firm's assets intact. It's not inconceivable that the partner killed him, but I'm sure as hell not going to the police about it with zero evidence. They're going to want to know why I'm interested. And my interest—and here's the ironic part—is that I was hired by you to keep the matter from going to the police. You want their help, be my guest. But that's where I get off."

"So you're writing me off?"

"I'm not doing anything of the kind. All I'm saying is Rubine, or whoever, seems to have bigger fish to fry. We'll give him a few weeks. In the meantime, there's nothing much to do but sit and hope he gets hit by a truck."

"But what if he goes to Butler?"

What the hell. If I didn't trust her now, I might as well

drop the case. She was holding out on me, that was for sure, but I didn't think she was doing so to harm me. If I explained things right, maybe she wouldn't get hysterical.

"Miss Lane, he *has* gone to Butler."

I heard a kind of "fffft" on the other end, a constricted kind of gasp.

"Good God."

"Now look, Miss Lane, you're still in good shape. All Butler knows is that somebody in his show made some films, but he doesn't know who."

"But he will know."

"Maybe yes, maybe no. By funny coincidence, Butler called me to get the films back for him."

"You're working for him?"

"I'm working for me, Miss Lane. He paid me real money to get those movies, but all he wants is to get this guy off his back. And that's all you want, or do you want something else?"

"No." Her voice was very, very small.

"Okay. Now you and Butler want the films back. If I pick up the films, there's a very good chance nobody will ever see them. If you want I can destroy the prints and screw up the negatives so badly that Butler couldn't tell you from Minnie Mouse, if he wanted to make prints from them. If he does want prints, then I don't know what the hell kind of a deal he's pulling. As far as I know, he wants to pay somebody off and keep his good name as a gentleman of Broadway."

"God, you're so rational, Mr. LeVine."

"Private dicks aren't known for being great abstract thinkers, Miss Lane, but we can get around town without a map. Now I'll try and speak to you on Monday. Spend the weekend with your boyfriend; go boating in the park or something. Just don't drive yourself nuts over this. We'll find a way out."

"Thanks for everything, Mr. LeVine."

"I haven't done anything but walk into some empty rooms."

"No," and she still sounded very scared, "you've been a real comfort."

"That's very kind. Good night, and take it easy."

Butler's receptionist waved me right into the main office. "He's expecting you."

I knocked once and walked in. Butler was at his little wall safe.

"Here for your winnings, Jack?" I got the marquee smile.

"Something like that." I settled myself into one of those burgundy chairs and lit up a cigarette. "Mr. Butler, do you know a Philadelphia banker named Eli W. Savage?"

Butler had his back to me, reaching deep into the safe.

"Excuse me, Jack. One second." He pulled out some bills and closed the safe and pushed the Gershwin picture back to the wall. When he walked back to the desk, I realized that he had a slight twitch in his eyelid. I hadn't noticed that the first time.

"Now, you said something about a banker." He sat down.

"Yes. Eli W. Savage, from Philadelphia. When I was going through the Smithtown house, I found this clipping." I got up and handed the newspaper photo to Butler. "It's a long shot. I thought you might have heard of the guy."

Butler stared at the picture for a few seconds. "Yes, I met him once about five years ago, at a party. It was after the Philadelphia opening of a show of mine called *The Rainbow Hunters*. But that's the only time, I believe. He's a big man in Philadelphia. You thought this picture might be important?"

"Beats me what I thought, Mr. Butler. It was the only

thing left in the house and it was obviously cut out for a reason."

Butler smiled. "Maybe this man is blackmailing Mr. Savage."

"Could be. Or Mr. Dewey."

"Yes," and Butler started laughing, "yes indeed, Mr. Dewey. For making improper advances to a gangster."

It was a pretty funny thought.

"Actually," Butler said, leaning back in his chair and fiddling with a pencil, "Mr. Savage is a substantial contributor to the Republican Party. Blackmailing him would be pretty juicy, I'd imagine."

I took a look at all those pictures of Butler with Farley, Lehman, and FDR.

"You must help out the Democrats quite a bit from the looks of those pictures. That's pretty classy company."

"Oh, Farley's not so classy." Butler tugged at his ear. "But FDR is a great man, Jack, and I'm proud to help the Democratic party any way I can. They saved this country and the whole free enterprise system back in 1933. That's what nobody understands anymore; without FDR, there would have been a real revolution in the United States and we'd all be up the creek without a paddle." Butler was getting a little agitated. He had leaned forward and was softly beating the desk with his left hand, emphasizing his points. "My old man died because those mines weren't supervised properly, because he had to work twelve hours a day, because nobody gave a good goddamn about people like him. But now everybody forgets about that, forgets that there could have been a Red takeover. All they can do is bitch about the reforms he did make. People forget very fast in this country."

I thought I'd push him a bit.

"Roosevelt got us into this goddamn war."

"That's infamous!" Butler screamed, half rising from his seat. The veins in his neck stood out so much you could

51

count them. "I'll throw you out on your ear, you goddamn tinhorn shamus."

"You didn't let me finish, Mr. Butler. I was saying that I'd heard people on the street say that, hackies, barbers, newsies, average Joes. They think FDR knew all along that we were going to get involved."

"Well, they're wrong." He ran his hands through his silver hair. "I'm sorry I blew up like that, Jack. You found my weak spot. I guess that's the mark of a good detective."

"That's what they taught us in detective school."

He nodded distantly. "Well, let's give you your money." His composure had returned as suddenly as it had departed. I watched him count five twenties and held out my hand to receive them.

"Maybe this case is over or maybe it's just suspended," Butler said, "while our 'Friend of the Arts' is chasing after bankers or whatever. God only knows. That clipping you brought is intriguing, but I'm not sure if it ties in anywhere."

"Either am I," I told him. "It hardly even qualifies as a long shot."

"Yes," he said, a little vaguely, as if he wasn't quite sure what I was saying. "In any case I'll keep you informed of anything that might arise, and I'm confident you'll do the same for me."

"For two-hundred fish, you can count on it."

Butler stood up, which meant he had had enough of me. "That's all I ask, Jack. Just keep me informed. All my life I've kept on top of things and it has brought me this." He waved his arm around the office. "And I'm not letting anybody," and his voice dropped to a whisper, "*any*body, take it from me." I was getting a ham hero with everything on it, but managed to keep a straight face.

"I don't think anybody said they were going to take away your office, Mr. Butler." Eileen opened the door and held it there. Time to go. "Afternoon." I turned and walked out, chucking the redhead under her chin.

"Stay as sweet as you are, Eileen."

"Get lost," she said, showing me all four rows of teeth.

I left the Schubert Building feeling a little like a mogul and the uniformed turkey downstairs smiled at me—doormen and guards can judge how much is in your wallet by the way you walk or something. It's uncanny. I decided to hold on to the cash rather than stick it in my office safe, figuring it would help intimidate the boys at the poker table that evening. When three Sunnyside low-stakes gamblers get a whiff of sawbucks in the air, their game gets affected. It has to.

Which is why I only lost five bucks that evening, at least two or three below par for me. I'm not the most effective poker player in the world for the simple reason that I smile whenever I get a good hand. It's what they call a reflex. So the hundred didn't do me all that much good on Friday night.

But it did me a lot of good on Saturday, beginning at 3:00 A.M., when I heard soft pounding on my door and someone whispering, "Mr. LeVine, Mr. LeVine. Jack LeVine?" I got up slowly, not all that sure I was hearing right, but the beating on my door got more insistent and I didn't want to wake up the whole building. Peering through the peephole was, as always, useless, and I was so foggy and crusty-eyed that I wouldn't have recognized Rita Hayworth standing naked in the hall. It wasn't Rita anyhow. It was some guy who asked me to please let him in because he had to talk with me. He realized it was a funny hour but his life was in great danger. Another hour and he might be dead. I wasn't sure that I was doing anything right but I let the guy in.

He said his name was Al Rubine.

I UNLOCKED THE DOOR and Rubine came through it like he'd
been shot out of a circus cannon. He went to the living-room
window, opened the venetian blinds a little, and looked down
into the street, just like in the movies. He was breathing
hard and perspiring like a guy laying asphalt at high noon.

"Thanks for letting me in, Jack. I appreciate it." He sat
down on the living-room couch, took off his hat and turned my
big three-way lamp to low. I just stood and looked at him,
still more asleep than awake.

"I'll make some coffee," I told him and somnambulated
into the kitchen, trailing the cord of my white terry-cloth
robe. I fussed with the kettle, got a high flame going and stuck
my head out of the kitchen archway to size Rubine up. He sat
short and squat in dark slacks, an open sport shirt, and tan
lightweight sport jacket. A pinkie ring adorned his left hand.
He had a few black hairs combed carefully across his head,
but in a stiff wind he'd be as bald as I am. Rubine's high-
cheekboned face was a blank: his nose had been broken a few
times, his lips were thick, his skin sallow, and his eyes had
been turned off a long time ago. Al Rubine looked like a small-
time crook. And he was in my apartment at a quarter past
three in the morning, huffing and puffing like a marathon run-
ner, because he was a small-time crook who found himself
in the big time and wanted to get the hell out before he wasn't
in any kind of time at all. Rubine looked very unhappy sitting on the couch. I watched him slick back his side hair with
open palms and try and keep his hands still enough to light up
a cigarette.

The kettle let loose with a sharp whistle and I turned it
off before Mrs. Freundlich upstairs got concerned and started
sticking her head next to the steam pipe for a listen. I filled

54

the top of my "Dripmaster" with enough water for eight cups. It might be a long time before the sun came up and Rubine and I had finished.

"How do you like your coffee?" I called from the kitchen. "Light or dark, Rubine?"

"Black, no sugar. Call me Al."

"Al it is." I methodically set up two cups and saucers, trying to work myself awake before I started talking with this prince. Just to keep Rubine on his toes, I chucked him a question.

"Who's chasing you, Al?"

Rubine started and looked toward the kitchen. He ran his hands through his pockets a couple of times, like a mechanical man.

"Jack—mind if I call you Jack?" and he flashed an uncertain grin that started out a smile and ended up a grimace. "I can't talk this way, you in there and me out here perched like a goddamn canary. You come in here, Jack, we can talk, whaddya say?"

I grunted and sat down on a stool in the kitchen, listening to the coffee drip and looking out of the open window. It was still pretty warm and there was a full moon that cast rays of pale, thin light on the roofs of Sunnyside. No cars were moving, the street lamps were all alone, and the block was so still and sweet that it was almost worth being up. Almost. I guess I couldn't kick. If I lived in London, I'd look out my window and see nothing but ruins. All I had to worry about was a nervous blackmailer playing with his cuffs in my living room. I waited, jiggled the top part of the coffee pot and filled two cups with steaming java, putting a little sugar in mine. By the time I paraded out to the living room like a good host, I was almost awake.

"I'm here. So who's chasing you, Al, and why'd you come to me?" I put the cups on the coffee table, sat down in an overstuffed chair to the right of the couch and lit up a Lucky.

55

"Second part first, okay Jack?" The smile was fast and thin, like a neon sign on the skids. "I came to you because there's a poor lady lives next door to me in Smithtown. When I pull out the other night, I tell her to let me know if I get visitors and who they are. I give her a number where she can reach me and fifteen bucks."

"I only gave her five."

The smile lasted a little longer this time. Rubine's teeth were as big and yellow as Seabiscuit's. "That's why she told on you."

I shrugged, a good loser. "Must be. I can't blame her, she looked like she hadn't seen much dough lately, if ever."

"I'm with you all the way on that." Rubine lifted his cup and let the steam fill his broken nose. "Prosit, Jack." He sipped the coffee very delicately. "Delicious, my compliments to the chef."

I yawned a little more sleep out of my system and swallowed some coffee. It was excellent. "You still haven't told me who's chasing you, Al."

"Everybody."

"I was supposed to meet you yesterday—rather, I was supposed to meet somebody called 'Friend of the Arts' yesterday—and pick up some stag films. All I found was a picture of Dewey and a banker."

He was going to take another sip, but his hands got a little shaky and he put his cup down. "Sounds interesting."

"Fascinating, in fact. But where the hell were you?"

"At a place you can be in a couple of hours, if you'll take me. I'd like to go and you'd like those films."

"You stashed the films in another hideout? Why?"

Rubine tried the coffee again but his hands didn't work and it spilled onto his pants.

"Jack, let me tell you straight," the words came out in a rush. "All I want is to get my ass into Canada before I get croaked. The films are yours, I don't give a shit. See, this pal of mine and me got in a blackmail scheme and we were backed up by some very big people who needed some big things done. We were just messenger boys, I swear to Christ."

"The other guy was Fenton."

"On the nose, Jack. Duke Fenton. Duke started figuring he could put the squeeze on these guys, and got killed so fast that it's positively scary. Get me? I figure I'm in for the same treatment on account of being Duke's partner and knowing the story." He leaned forward. "Jack, I could put the finger on so many people your hair would stand on end."

"I don't have any hair."

"Your scalp then." He just said it. He wasn't even trying to make with the jokes. "The way I see it, Duke and I were set up for suckers the day we got hired. When Duke got cute, it just meant he got the payoff first."

"Al, who are these guys?"

Rubine shook his head.

"Jack, you're a nice guy but you could make a fast bundle of cash letting them know where I was. I can't tell you that. I hardly know you, for Crissakes."

"How much dough you figure I could get by turning you in?"

"The kind of dough where you could move from Sunnyside to Park Avenue, that much dough."

"I like Sunnyside, but I know what you mean."

"You're not so dumb." Rubine slapped my knee. There was a lot of perspiration on his upper lip and he needed a shave. "Just kidding, Jack. You're one of the smartest guys in the business."

"I was coming to that. What do you want from me?"

"Not from, Jack, for. I want you to drive me to New Kingston, New York, that's five, five and a half hours from here. There I got the films stashed away in a farmhouse that Fenton's aunt lives in. I left my car in Margaretville. That's five miles away. You get the films, I pick up my car and disappear."

"Why didn't you drive down here?"

"I was afraid of getting tailed to your house. Nobody's tailed me yet but it's bound to happen and I'm scared for real, pallie. So I dropped the car off on a side street in Margaretville and caught the late bus down here. It's summer season starting, so they run a couple of buses to the city every day."

Rubine was filling me with useless information. With my brain still clumsy, I groped for the right questions before getting completely lost.

"Al, why are you giving me those films?"

"I can't think of nobody else, sweetheart." He had a lot of things to call people. "You're an interested party, right? You were the guy came all the way out to Smithtown, so take 'em. And it's a nice ride up there."

"At 3:30?"

"It gets light out early these days."

I had nothing better to do and after three cups of potent coffee I could have gone over Niagara in a barrel faster than I could have gone back to sleep, so I shuffled into the bedroom and got dressed in brown corduroy pants, a yellow pullover sport shirt, my ancient khaki jacket, and a camel-colored cap. When I returned to the living room, Rubine was all ready and waiting by the door. And pointing a gun in the general direction of LeVine's generous and forgiving heart.

"Goddamn son of a bitch," I said, angrier at myself than at Rubine.

"Hey, don't get mad, pallie, it's just too risky without. Like I said, you could make a lot of dough taking me to the right people."

"Especially if I don't know who they are."

"Maybe you don't, maybe you do. What do I know, right? Put yourself in my position; you got to watch yourself, am I right?"

"You're afraid I'll take you to the cops. That's it, isn't it, Al? You probably had a thousand reasons for knocking off Fenton. Once they grabbed you, the case would be closed."

"Sure. That's why I'm giving you the films, because I wanted them so bad that I killed my own partner for them. You're talking stupid, Jack."

"Maybe you wanted the films all for yourself and then found you were in too deep. Maybe you're not giving me the films at all. Maybe you're just a prick who likes to flash guns around." I turned my head to the right very fast and suckered Rubine into doing the same, giving me the chance to grab his wrist with both hands and slam it into the steel doorknob. The gun fell to the floor and Rubine didn't even go for it.

"It isn't loaded, Jack," he said, looking like a dog caught crapping on the rug.

"Then you're a bigger schmuck than I thought, Al. You can get hurt threatening people with empty guns." I put the little Colt in my pants pocket. "You still want to go to New Kingston, or is this going to spoil the whole trip for you?"

Rubine rubbed his wrist and shook his head. "No, I still want to go. Last night, I realized I didn't have anything to put in the gun. And I need it, believe me. I'm not being chased by no nuns." He stared at me with sad brown eyes. "This might sound stupid after what just happened, but could you lend me a little ammo?"

"How about I just give you five thousand bucks to buy some and trust you for the change. Let's get out of here already."

"I'm serious, Jack buddy."

"Maybe I'll help you out once I've got the films and you're ready to scram over the border. But nix until then, Al. I seem to remember your once pulling a gun on me."

He ran his left hand through his bit of hair and stuck the injured hand in his jacket pocket for a rest. "Don't think I don't understand, Jack." He fussed with his collar. The guy was scared, that was no act. But he was as predictable as a hophead in the five-and-ten. "I just don't want you to think I don't understand," he repeated.

"I think you understand. Okay?" I nodded toward the door and he opened it. I shut the lights and locked up. We walked down two flights of stairs into the quiet little blue-and-marble lobby of my building and out to the street. The sky had lightened almost imperceptibly, from black-blue to blue-black. It was nearing four o'clock and except for one gray tomcat, the street was as deserted as the far side of the moon.

"Christ, you can hear yourself think," Rubine said.

"Can you hear anything?"

"Hey Jack, don't break my balls. Things are bad enough, I don't need that."

"I'll be a regular angel, you'll see. My car's across the street, the white Buick." We walked over and I opened the door on the driver's side. Rubine slid in, lit up a cigarette and started whistling "It's Only a Shanty in Old Shantytown" while I started the engine. We embarked: two unlikely playmates off to New Kingston, New York, at 3:55 A.M. on a Saturday morning. You figure it out.

I'ts A LONG TIME getting up to the Catskill mountain region where Rubine had stashed Kerry Lane's films. Not an unpleasant drive, to be sure. On a brilliant afternoon in May with a good woman, it's probably a hell of a way to spend your time. Before dawn, with a whistling blackmailer afflicted with bad breath and the fear that most people wanted to kill him, it was something less than a joyride.

"You probably want to know how I got into this racket," Rubine said as we entered the Palisades Parkway in New Jersey—a right turn off George and Martha Washington's bridge. He hadn't said anything until then, about forty minutes, and I'd hoped he was asleep.

"Not unless you're going to tell me about this case, Al."

"I might," he said, suddenly cheered by the knowledge that he did, after all, have some information of use to me, suddenly feeling like something more than a third-rate shyster on the lam. "I might if you're good to me."

"What do you want me to do, lick your ear?"

He lit up an Old Gold. "Jack, stop being a goddamned hardboiled egg and enjoy yourself. I can do you some favors."

"So do them. Why were all those newspapers scattered around that house in Smithtown? You working for the War Department on the side?"

Rubine started coughing and managed to rasp out, "Hit my back," which I did until he wheezed and hocked to a stop.

"Wheew. Smoke went down the wrong pipe." He coughed quietly a few times, his face going from red to white, like one of those fancy jukeboxes with the swirling color changes.

"Al, the newspapers. You were going to help me out."

"Not on that, pallie. You'll figure it out, though. It won't take you long. Not a guy with your rep."

"You're making me blush."

Rubine chuckled.

"You know how I got into this racket?" he said again, like it was the first line of a song. "Funny thing, I hardly know myself." He shook his head, in acknowledgement of the mysteries of life. "How old you think I am?"

"Eleven."

"Come on, serious."

I took a quick look.

"Mid-forties."

"I'm thirty-five years old, Jack. Ain't that a pisser? Thirty-five years old."

"You don't look so hot, Al."

"That's for goddamn sure. I been going with this tomato for four years. When she met me, I had a full head of hair. Now you can use my scalp for a mirror. All the time she's on me about it. Wants me to get a toup. You get that, Jack? About the hair? You're a little thin up there. You got a girl bothers you about that?"

"No. She likes it. Reminds her of a beloved uncle."

"Well, you're a lucky guy."

"That's what everybody tells me."

"Yeah. I got to agree with them." Rubine fell silent, then cranked up his life story again. "When I was eighteen, eighteen years of age, I left New York and went to Detroit to help my Uncle Irv, who was bringing in hooch from Canada. I was a dumb kid from Bensonhurst and that was just fabulous back then." His voice grew soft and wistful. "Plenty of cabbage, plenty of broads, house right on the lake. Private dock. Sound good?"

"Fabulous."

"I don't know if you're serious or not, Jack. It's hard to tell with you." Rubine shook his head, trying to figure out why I was such a bastard. He gave up and went on: "Then Prohibition ended and we were out on our asses. No more broads, no more parties, no more house right on the lake. A lot of shines were starting to move into Detroit, so Uncle Irv figured he'd get some action on the numbers and loan-sharking. But he didn't figure fast enough and wound up in the driver's seat of a Chevy parked on the bottom of Lake Superior."

"Tough break."

"He was a great guy, my Uncle Irv, a straight shooter. Not like this son of a bitch I've been working for."

I was quiet and Rubine picked up the note of expectancy in that silence, and realized he was talking too much. He lit up another cigarette and inadvertantly blew some smoke across my face. I coughed.

"Jesus, Jack, I'm sorry. I thought you were a smoker."

"I am." But he had already thrown his Old Gold out the window.

"When you're driving, it's tough enough without people gassing you, am I right?" Rubine asked, and despite myself, I was really starting to feel sorry for this poor little chump. So full of apologies and regrets. A born pawn. A born messenger boy.

"So to make a long story short, I just got out of Detroit pronto after Irv was nailed and came back to New York. That's ten, eleven years ago. And ever since, it's been a buck here, a buck there. But never like it was in Detroit. I ain't had it that good since."

"That goes for everybody, Al. Everyone has a Detroit somewhere along the line and then it all turns to vinegar."

He shook his head very gravely, like I had just summed it up for the whole universe, and said no more. A few minutes later, we were entering Route 9W and Rubine fell asleep.

He slept like a baby for the next couple of hours. The sun was rising when I turned off 9W for the last leg of the journey to New Kingston.

Which is when I noticed the patrol car.

I wasn't going much faster than forty-five as I got on Route 28, but there was a red glare bouncing off my rear view mirror. The car's light was flashing and I saw a beefy arm extending out the driver's window. The arm was waving for me to pull over. There was no siren, just the flashing red light. And the arm.

When I pulled over to the side of the road and stopped, Rubine woke up.

"What's going on?" he yawned.

"The law."

Rubine turned a further shade of pale and started shaking as I turned to see a very big man with blue jowls, dark glasses and a wide trooper's hat leaning in through my window.

"Way too fast, mister. Way too fast."

"Forty-five is way too fast?"

"That's correct." He had a hard, flat voice, a disinterested voice. His partner came over: a medium-sized man with shoulders you could use for a dance floor. He was also wearing a trooper's hat and dark glasses.

"Everybody's wearing glasses," I said, making pleasant conversation.

"Both of you gentlemen please step out of the car," said the tall trooper. The other stood maybe five paces behind him, his arms folded across a wide chest.

Al Rubine looked at me like a trapped animal. There was a note in the sound of the trooper's command that didn't have anything to do with speeding tickets. Maybe these guys really were troopers, but I wouldn't have laid a dime on it.

"Jack, we got to get out of here," Rubine whispered.

"Please, both you gentlemen step out of the car." Rubine whimpered, there's no other way to describe the sound he made, and pushed open his door. He was rubbing his jaw, like he expected to get hit there. I got out and hitched up my pants, like I was a tough guy.

"Both of you gentlemen on this side of the car, please," the tall trooper stated. He sounded as matter-of-fact as a stock clerk doing inventory.

"Backs to us, please, facing the vehicle, and hands in the air."

Rubine came over and stood next to me, slowly raising his hands in the air. His eyes had switched off and his face was drawn and rigid, with a left eyelid that wouldn't stop twitching. Except for the twitch, he would have looked fine on a taxidermist's wall.

"Search them," said the tall trooper. I felt hands going through my pockets, lightly and professionally. The hands found my gun and Rubine's empty Colt and removed them.

"Both you gentlemen please take one step away from the vehicle, arms still raised."

I don't scare easy, but I was very scared now. Rubine whimpered again and I heard a suppressed grunt and the sound of a twisting foot behind me and turned my head. Turned it much too late. I felt a sharp sting behind my left ear and the world turned bright red and blue. Lightning went through my head and I felt strangely legless, as if only the top half of my body were falling. I was talking to the door of the car and felt something fall beside me, as I sank beneath layer upon layer of lukewarm water. My brain was talking to itself and I tried hard to listen in, but it got very far away and my head hurt so badly. The rocks were pearly and my lips pressed against the Buick's hubcaps.

I was out.

THE BACK OF MY NECK was on fire and a midget roller derby was being held in my stomach. Orange-green flashbulbs kept exploding outside my closed lids. When I got my eyes open, a flood of sunlight blew my head apart and triggered an immediate swell of nausea. I breathed heavily to fight off the inevitable, inhaling soil and pollen, turning my head with effort, glistening with cold sweat. A mighty sneeze sent an ant flying from my nostril, like a kid chuting out of the Coney Island funhouse. The sneeze hurt all over and I breathed deeply once again, holding on just barely, tottering near the edge and finally calling it quits. I wrenched my head to the side and threw up. LeVine starts his weekend.

I felt terribly weak, but the roller derby was winding down and the ache wasn't so bad. I got to my knees, tore up some weeds and wiped my mouth, and remembered where I was: in some high grass a hundred feet from the highway, hidden from the sight of motorists. My car sat placidly on the road shoulder. A bread truck rattled past, raising dust that went up and up and seemed to settle in the clouds. A bright, scrubbed morning. Everything was peaceful, everything was simple—until I remembered why I was here, and who I had come with. Maybe they had put him in the back seat of the car. Sure. Maybe they had bought him dinner and given him a gold watch.

So I was a detective again, rising from the earth and stalking toward the car with the easy grace of Frankenstein's monster carrying a piano upstairs. I tripped in some tangled weeds, caressed my shin on a stone and squealed in pain, limping the last thirty feet. My shirt was soaked through and I sat down heavily in the front seat of my patient Buick. I was panting.

Rubine, of course, wasn't in the car. Chances were he was eyeball to eyeball with a lake trout, like his Uncle Irv. I leaned stiffly against the open door and noticed some drag marks in the dirt, made by a pair of limp heels. They ran along the side of the road for about fifty feet, so I followed the trail until it came to an abrupt end at a point on the concrete road where some freshly burnt rubber lay scattered about. Somebody had been in a hurry. I didn't think it was Rubine.

Not with those bloodstains.

I hadn't noticed any blood on the dusty stretch running parallel to the road, but this drying pool on the road made it pretty clear that my brief friendship with Rubine had come to an end. I wasn't particularly happy about it. Or unhappy. It made me nervous. I did my little sleuthing bit and found some stiff, flaky drops of dried blood along the path of the heel marks. Figuring some mug had carried Rubine with his hands hooked under the deceased's arms, it seemed certain he was going to have to change his shirt.

A small pick-up truck wheezed along the road and came to a stop beside me. I stuck my hand in my pocket and ducked as a wiry, nut-brown farmer leaned out the window and nodded in the direction of the Buick.

"Trouble?" His voice was husky and pleasant.

"The car's in better shape than I am."

"Uh, huh," he said neutrally, looking me over. "Thought you might need a push. Happens to the best."

"No, I'm just fine." I stuffed my hands into my back pockets and tried to be just folks. "You know how far I might be from New Kingston?"

"New Kingston." He thought about it. "New Kingston. 'Bout fifteen miles. What you do, stay on 28 and take her into Margaretville, go down Main Street and take your right by the drugstore. That's New Kingston Road they call it. Follow that three–four miles and you're in business."

"Fifteen miles altogether."

"Fifteen to Margaretville, then five. Say twenty." He kept

looking at me, so I wiped my hand across my brow and came up with some dried blood.

"You're okay?"

"I'm dandy. And thanks for the help."

"Sure," he said, grinding the gears into first and starting back west on 28. "That's by the drugstore," he called out. I waved, he took a corner and disappeared from view and it was quiet again. It was half past eight and already very warm. I brushed myself off, wiped away the crumbs of blood with a hanky, slipped into the Buick and started on down the road. I had made another mistake.

Margaretville was a movie house, a hardware store, a grocery, a clothing-and-notions emporium with aisles you had to walk down sideways, a firehouse, a gas station—and the drugstore. Farther down Main Street, a flag hung still against a windless blue sky and that was the post office. Farmers and farmers' wives were doing some early Saturday morning shopping, the old-timers sat on a bench in front of the hardware, mutts chased each other around. It was neat, bright, and orderly and my reasons for being there suddenly seemed outlandish. Stag films hidden up here? Fenton would have suffocated in the fresh air. This wasn't his world: he was more comfortable in hotels where guys peed down the dumbwaiters and dried their socks over hot plates. Margaretville was stepping out of a Lionel train into Anytown.

I parked on Main and walked to the drugstore, Christian's Drugstore to be exact. It was one of those places with orange Rexall bordering on the glass and displays of nickel toys. There was a nice poster in the window of a soldier and his girl drinking an ice cream soda together, two straws, while a white-haired guy in an apron watched approvingly, his arms folded across the fountain. "WHAT A HOMECOMING," it said.

Inside Christian's, the homecoming hadn't begun yet. A

forbidding-looking lady in her thirties stood behind a black marble-top counter while two old men in short-sleeve sport shirts talked of war.

"Japs could take the Russkies any day of the week," said a stringy man with an Adam's apple the size of a baseball.

"Course they could," said his pal, a chunky hayseed with eyeglasses as thick as milk bottles. "That's why we're doin' all the work. Jesus, I remember '04 like it was yesterday. Russkies never knew what hit 'em!"

"Old Teddy had to bail 'em out."

"That's right! Wasn't for Teddy, Japs would've finished 'em right off."

The lady stared at me as I surveyed the walls, looking for a phone book.

"You need help, mister, say so." Her voice was thin and taut: unwatered, unhugged. The old-timers put on the mutes and buried their noses in their coffee cups.

"I was looking for a phone book."

"Could've said so." She dipped her knees and pulled a thin booklet out from under the counter, a directory for Fleischmanns—Pine Hill—Margaretville.

"It's a New Kingston number."

"It'll be there, New Kingston's in there," the chunky man said.

There was one Fenton in the book—Mrs. Raymond Fenton, Thompson Hollow Road.

"Thompson Hollow Road," I said. "Where it is?"

"Who you looking for?" the lady said.

"Fenton."

"The Fenton place?" asked the Adam's apple. He looked at his friend and they both looked at Miss Christian behind the counter.

"You'll be the first visitor in a long while, mister," she said evenly. "Long, long while."

"She still live there?"

"Oh, she lives there all right. You want her, you'll find her." The lady poured herself a glass of water, keeping her eyes on me.

"She's just a strange kind of woman," the stout man said, trying to put me at my ease. He caught himself and got nervous. "You're not a relative, are you?"

"I represent people in her family. A small legal problem has to be cleared up."

"I see," said the Adam's apple. I don't think he believed a word of it.

"She live there alone?" I asked.

"Just her and a caretaker," the apple said. "He's the one you got to watch out for."

The lady behind the counter shot him a stern, reprimanding look.

"Man's got a right to know," he insisted. "Man's got a right to be warned."

I patted him on the shoulder. "I appreciate it, buddy."

The woman softened. "All right," she said, as if conceding a point. "Watch yourself. I think her boy's a convict. That's the word."

"She live up here long?"

She shook her head. "Five years."

"Moved into Pete Devereaux's house," said the chunky man. "Used to be a real showcase."

"Lord, yes," the Adam's apple nodded in assent. "It was the pride of the hollow." He sipped some coffee and it went down the wrong pipe. He launched into a small-scale coughing fit.

"Jesus Christ," he croaked, as the woman shoved her glass of water across the counter. Then she walked to the window.

"You really want to go there, you take this right turn right outside the store. Follow New Kingston Road all the way, bearing right as you go through New Kingston. Then it's the third left after the town."

"Thanks a lot," I said, pushing open the screen door and

looking at a Santa Claus Coca-Cola thermometer. Seventy-five degrees.

"Mister?" said the chunky man.

I turned toward him.

"Come back after you're finished. I swear you're the first man ever asked directions to that place."

I UNDERSTOOD WHY. The Fenton place was Halloween City, a huge, peeling-paint wooden mansion turned hovel with a spa-sized porch, turrets, parapets, broken weather vanes, and the high reek of decay. The dull gray exterior was practically skeletal: coat upon coat of paint had weathered away. The grounds were littered with rusted shapes that had once been farm implements. Weeds ran berserk, grass gave over to dandelion patches of a particularly drab and urinous yellow, shot up a foot high, and sped thick and untamed to the side of a stagnant brook. Swarms of mosquitoes tested my neck for tenderness. There was a lot of acreage, none of it used, cared for, or seemingly even recognized by its owner.

She had better things to do.

I was stooping to examine the rusted hulk of an anvil when I noticed a spidery little woman with brownish mottled skin staring at me through a screen door. I stood up and she turned away, then pushed open the door and walked across the porch. She was holding a rifle. It was for deer hunting. I was the deer.

"Git 'em up!" she screeched, her voice a fingernail drawn against a blackboard. "Berl!" she yelled back into the house. "BERL!!" she yelled more shatteringly. My hair stood up on my arms.

"Mrs. Fenton?"

At the far end of the long porch, another door opened and a huge blond boy–man, maybe twenty, maybe forty, came slowly out, majestically turning his head from me to the angry little woman, then back again.

"Berl, search!"

Berl eased himself down the stairs and walked slowly

across the grass in my direction. I didn't know that the Flat-iron Building could walk. Standing on ground level with Berl was humbling: if he didn't measure out to 6'8", 250, then I was Mighty Manuel, the Cuban midget.

He stopped a foot away and looked quizzically at me, his eyes so dull they could have been glass. He searched me. Rather, his hands searched me, big pale paws flopping mechanically but not without force, up and down my body. He found my gun and tossed it aside like a book of matches. Berl spoke:

"Okay search, Rose."

"Mrs. Fenton," I started.

"Shut up!" She came down the stairs, her rifle pointed roughly at a point equidistant from my left and right eyes.

"The gun isn't necessary," I tried, getting really worried.

"Berl, hit!" she screeched.

"Ah," he said and I was relieved until a fist the size of a melon came in a blur toward my stomach. I blocked it with my elbow and he chopped the back of my head—a spot already well-softened. I saw blue and green again and sat down in a heap. Berl moved very fast for a moron.

"Git up, Jewboy," said Aunt Rose.

I looked up at her raisin of a face and she smiled for the first time. A gracious and lovely woman.

"I can always tell a Jewboy. Always."

"The Germans could use you."

She stopped smiling. "Stand the hell up."

I got up and my head throbbed. A day in the country. "I was a friend of your nephew, Duke," I said lamely. It was the best I could do with my brains fast turning into Farina.

She laughed it off. "Duke was smart. He didn't have no friends, specially no Jewboys."

"If he's so smart, how come he's dead?"

"Got stabbed in the back. You know so much, you know that."

"By Al Rubine?"

She just stared at me. "Who? Listen, what are you, a cop?"

I shook my head. "I represent some people who were being shaken down by your beloved late nephew. There's a few things stored here that I'd like. Films. You'll be well paid."

"Get lost, mister. Whatever Duke left here, stays here. I got other irons in the fire; meantime, I'll sit on what I've got."

"Five thousand dollars wouldn't change your mind?"

"Show me five thousand dollars and I'll think about it."

"I can get it in twenty-four hours."

"You get it. We'll talk then."

I said it very fast: "About the Kerry Lane films."

"The what? . . ." she tried to stop herself.

"The films."

Her eyes betrayed her. She just nodded.

"Mrs. Fenton, are there any films here or not?"

Berl spoke. "Pictures, naked."

"Shut up," she spat.

"Still photos or movies, Berl, pictures that move?"

"Don't answer him, Berl."

"Mrs. Fenton, when's the last time Duke came up here?"

"A month ago," she said defensively. "He visit me regular, like a son."

A month ago didn't check at all. I had the crawly feeling that Rubine had been duped in more ways than one. Led up here on a blind and put away for keeps. Lied to by Fenton, lied to by everybody. Poor scared stupid little bastard.

"You want Berl again or you goin' to leave?"

"I'm leaving of my own volition, sweetheart."

"Hit?" asked Berl, a boy of simple pleasures.

"No, he's goin'."

I walked away and got into my car. My head hurt. Mrs. Fenton and Berl were staring at me and I was staring at them, trying to figure out what the hell was going on up here in New Kingston. Aunt Rose said something to Berl and he shouted, "No. No touch," stamped his feet and plodded back to the house, shaking his head heavily from side to side. I turned the key and the Buick gratefully took me away, first to tell the gang at Christian's that Mrs. Fenton was definitely a peculiar kind of broad and then to chew on a couple of poached eggs with potatoes, Canadian bacon, and four cups of coffee at a place outside Margaretville. It was nearing eleven and Rubine had walked in at three: eight hours that seemed like eight weeks. Country road workers were having an early lunch, while I finished breakfast at the end of my day, on my own clock in my own world, an alien visitor carrying out assignments on earth.

Four hours later, I was lazily floating in a Sunnyside bath-tub filled with darkening water, a Blatz loyally standing next to the tub. Mel Allen's honeyed tones wafted from the Philco, my phone was off its hook, and the Yanks were up 3–0 on the Athletics, scoring their runs off an eighteen-year-old 4-F south-paw who had two glass eyes and a mechanical leg. God was in his heaven. LeVine felt like a person for the first time in three days. After an hour of soaking, I arose, streaming, to shave and talcum myself, then called Kitty Seymour to ex-plain my recent whereabouts and shyly ask if she would tolerate having dinner with me.

"Your place or mine?" she asked.

"I thought I'd spring for it."

"You pay for it? Must be some case, Jack."

"It's rotting my mind. How about it?"

"Fact is I'm having some people over tonight and I made enough stew for the Russian front. Why not grace our table?"

"What kind of people?"

"Couple of War Information guys, very bright, one failed-nightclub-chanteuse-turned-dress-shop-owner, a house-wife or two. A higher grade of person than you usually run into."

"That's inconceivable, but I'll come anyhow. What time?"

"Seven-thirty. They're not a late crowd so the place will be ours by midnight."

"I'll probably be pretty tired but I could stay awake with encouragement."

"You'll get so much encouragement you won't know where to hide. See you."

I dressed slowly, as Mel Allen's voice grew cranky, less buoyant. In the bottom of the eighth, a four-fingered left fielder for the A's hit a grand slammer off a palsied Yank reliever. The A's, in turn, wheeled out a seventy-year-old southpaw who put the Yanks away nice and easy in the top of the ninth, and what sounded like two hundred people filed peacefully out of Shibe Park.

So when does DiMaggio get home already? Where he's needed.

The stew was delicious, the company stimulating, but I couldn't keep my eyes open and was happy when the last bye-byes went sailing past the closing doors. Kitty turned and smiled, her back to the door.

"Now, they weren't *that* boring!"

"Not in the least. I've just been up since three o'clock this morning, drove up and down from the country—five hours each way, got slugged twice, once with a sap, had a traveling companion killed, and was threatened myself."

"So you're tired."

"So I'm tired."

Kitty stepped toward me. Her lipstick was very red and her brown hair was pulled back. She looked very beautiful, like Ann Sheridan, for whom I was keeping myself. Kitty put her hands on my rosy cheeks and stretched her long fingers so that they smoothed my scalp.

"I love running my fingers through your hair," she said.

"Last dame made a crack about my dome went to bed with a T-bone pressed to her eye."

"Tough guy." Kitty stepped even closer so that all I could see was her. It made the world a very pretty place. I softly kissed her eyes and her nose, then landed on her warm and fragrant mouth.

"Kitty, you're all right," I told her ear.

It was a fine, sweet night, the nicest since my divorce, maybe the nicest since the middle of my marriage. There was energy, softness, grace, and laughter. I even took my socks off. In my circle, that means class.

12

I'M CRAZY FOR DICK TRACY. I think he's a hell of a guy who does his job the way I've always wanted to do mine: square-jawed and full steam ahead, undeterred by extraneous difficulties. I'm not like that. In 1938, for instance, I was following a pretty important guy around, an actor (you'd know the name) whose wife was trying to nail him pants down for a divorce suit. I ate some bad potato salad for lunch, got the runs, and repeatedly lost the guy. No sooner would he turn into an apartment building, push a buzzer, and go inside than a familiar pang would shiver through my kishkas and I'd be streaking into a luncheonette or a barbershop, racing toward the back. I've never, ever, seen that happen to Tracy, or to B.O. and Sparkle Plenty, who also do their bits. As for Tracy's sidekick, Pat Patton, I wish he worked with me; I could use a tough Irishman on my side. And his eyes seem to twinkle. Especially on Sundays, in color.

Especially this Sunday. Kitty and I enjoyed a sleepy, giggly kind of breakfast, poring over the *News* and *Mirror*. She made breakfast; I insisted on doing the dishes. She came up behind me as I faced the sink, and wrapped her arms around me and held me very tight. I dried my hands and we went off to the bedroom once again. At about noon, I left.

"Now that you've compromised me yet again, Jack, I expect you'll call," Kitty told me at the door.

I pinched her cheek, a happy guy.

"You'll get flowers and candy by the carload."

It was a drizzly Sunday and the streets were empty. I splurged and took a cab to Sunnyside, studying the closed stores, the gray East River, and my contented visage as reflected in driver Meyer Domoff's rear-view mirror.

A peaceful Sunday afternoon. Lots of time to peruse the papers, sip more coffee and enjoy the easy warmth of my limbs the post-lovemaking glow. An item in the *News* caught my eye, if not my fancy.

BODY FOUND

Olive, N.Y. June 23 (AP)—Police here report the discovery of an unidentified body late this afternoon, near Esopus Creek in Olive. Sheriff Walter Runstead said the body of a forty-year-old white male was discovered jammed into a wide section of drainpipe northwest of the creek. "We've ascertained that death occurred within the past twenty-four hours," Runstead reported. Cause of death was not disclosed. The Kingston Police Department promised later details.

So long, Al.

I turned my radio on and let some Mozart into the morning. Which is when I got my first treat of the day. The phone rang and I answered with a mouth full of toast.

"Hello?"

"LeVine?"

"Uh-hmm."

"Get the hell off this case or you'll join your friend Rubine. It wasn't nice what they did to him. Be smart." The voice was a hoarse rasp.

"It wasn't nice what they did to me. My head still aches."

"They was nice to you, LeVine. Believe me."

The connection wasn't too good—there was a lot of crackle over the wire. "You calling long-distance?"

"Get off the case, buster. Or it'll hurt." He hung up.

I leafed through the Entertainment section of the *News*. There was a new Betty Grable film, *Pin-Up Girl*. Maybe I'd go see it for a couple of months. They have bathrooms in theaters. I decided to call Butler at home. If they wanted me off the case, chances were he'd been told the same thing. Or would be, so I could warn him. A young man answered.

"You can be a star, good morning."

"Let me talk to Butler, sweetie."

"The master is indisposed. Who shall I say?"

"Say Jack LeVine."

"The *dick?*" he asked. His hand was either on his hip or sweeping across his bangs. He sounded adorable.

"*The* dick."

I heard him calling Butler: "Warren, your dick is on the phone." The young man covered the mouthpiece, and I heard dulled shouts; then he spoke again.

"He's been a perfect bitch all morning."

"Happens in the best of marriages."

"How very true."

Butler grabbed the phone, sounding upset. "Jack, I'm glad you called."

"I like your friend."

"Jack, I've been threatened and it was damn ugly. This morning."

"By phone?"

"Yes."

"They've really been cranking out the calls this morning. My life was declared worthless just a few minutes ago."

"God, they called you, too?"

"Told me to get off the case or I'd be cross-ventilated. What did they tell you."

"To take you off the case."

"Or?"

"Or they'd make it rough on me."

"How, physically?"

He faltered. "I assume so. They just said, 'Well make it rough on you.'"

"A man with a raspy kind of voice."

"That's right. What do you make of this, Jack?"

"It's nuts. First they want a contact to make a deal. I go to Smithtown, nothing. Now they're playing tough."

"It is quite strange. I don't like it."

"And you don't know the half of it. Yesterday morning

at 3:00 A.M. our friend Rubine, late of Smithtown and the universe, came to my apartment on the lam. He told me to drive upstate, where I'd find the films in a farmhouse. He was a scared little guy. I drive him up and when we hit Route 28, a patrol car tails us and pulls us over. We get out, put our hands up and then a piano fell on my head. I wake up, Rubine's gone and there's blood all over the road."

"Jack, please." Butler sounded ill.

"Life isn't nice, Butler. I'm sorry about it but you hired me to tell you things and I'm telling them to you."

"I understand, but not so graphic, please."

"That's the only ugly part; the rest is low comedy. I keep going, schmuck that I am, and visit the farmhouse where Duke Fenton, Rubine's ex-partner, stashed the films. I get there and a fifty-year-old woman holds a gun on me and sends over a seven-foot caretaker to play catch with my head. Net result after all the heavy stuff was that she knew nothing from nothing. Another net result is a little item in the *News* this morning, saying that an unidentified stiff was found doing the Australian crawl in a drainage pipe near where I got sapped. Figures to be Rubine."

"And this all happened yesterday?"

"Big day."

"And why didn't you call me when you got back?" He sounded angry. "I hired you, why the hell do I have to call and pump information from you? I'm buying information, Jack."

"Hold on. First of all, I would have told you eventually. In fact, I just told you about it, willingly and, I thought, pithily. I remember you telling me to stop at one point. Second of all, it's a funny story but it doesn't get us any further; probably takes us back a couple of paces. Third and last, by the time I got home yesterday I hardly knew which end of the phone to use. I'd been hit on the head a few times, like I said."

"Sorry, Jack, it's no lack of faith on my part. This has just been . . . " his voice started to break, "very upsetting."

"Look, just lay low for a bit. Don't move around any more than necessary. We're up against a very rough bunch of people and worse than that, a very unpredictable bunch. You know anybody who packs a gun?"

"Yes."

"Okay. Keep him with you."

"And you, Jack?"

"I'm paid to stick my neck out."

The next step, of course, was to call Kerry and warn her, and I cursed myself for not forcing a phone number out of her. She could be in really terrible danger and her failure to call did little to reassure me. I would have to sweat it out until the next day, when I could at least call the theater and leave a message. For now, I would try and pretend it was just another Sunday in June; nobody had slugged me and I was just a stocky Queens Jew sitting around in his underwear.

So it was sunday for a while. The Yankees split a pair and
LeVine split a half-dozen beers with Irv Rapp from 3D,
diagonally across the hall from me. Irv's in hats. We talked
about the old days, wished they were back. Irv's doing well,
got a sub-contract on sailor caps and swears he'll buy a Packard
when the war's over. Kitty called and we had a giggly, incon-
clusive talk, like two twenty-year-olds sharing breakfast after
their first night in the sack.

Which brought me to Monday.

Monday when the whole Kerry Lane case started to make
perfect and incredible sense.

Monday when I wished it hadn't.

I walked into 1651 Broadway at about 9:30, insulted the
elevator jockey, and unlocked my office door a lot more carefully than usual. The outer office was unoccupied and untouched, but I suddenly heard a rattling noise in the inner
sanctum. I turned the key as quietly as possible, then leaned
against the door with my full weight, drew my Colt and burst
inside, yelling, "What the hell . . ." at the source of the noise.
Predictably, there was no reply. The metal piece at the end of
the window shade continued to rap against the window pane,
blown about by my electric fan, which I had neglected to shut
off. I cleared my throat and returned the Colt to my pocket.

It was at least an hour too early to call the theater so I
killed time by reading the papers—Tracy was zeroing in on a
mastermind killer with a deformed head—and answering some
calls. An advertising man from Darien was sure that his wife
was taking care of the private school headmaster in the after-
noons and wanted his house staked out. I told him no dice and
gave him the numbers of a couple of shamuses who were good,

needed a buck, and enjoyed that type of work. He told me how much he loved his wife.

At eleven I rang backstage at the Booth and asked to leave a message for Kerry Lane. I was asked to hang on and was given over to an assistant stage manager. This time I asked if Kerry was around.

"Not right now, Mac."

"Can I leave a message?"

"That wouldn't make much sense."

I got annoyed. "It makes sense if there's no other way to reach her."

"No, it don't make sense because she left the show."

I watched a couple of file clerks pick their teeth across the air shaft and was surprised at how hard my heart was beating.

"Hello? You still on, Mac?"

"When did she leave the show?"

"This morning. Called up and said she had to go home— somebody in the family's sick."

"So she's out for good?"

"That's what I wanted to know. Kerry said she'd try and come back in a few weeks, but she wasn't sure."

"How'd she sound, nervous?"

There was a pause and I heard breathing. He was thinking. "Is this the law?"

"Private investigator. Kerry hired me to take care of something."

"She in trouble?"

"Nothing serious. Look, you have any idea where she might be headed?"

"Not really, but I figured she might be from around Philly. Something she said once. We were on the road in Boston and she asked me a couple of times if there was any chance of us playing Philly."

"And you got the idea she wasn't very anxious to go there, that it?"

"That's it. You're pretty good. I had the feeling that if

I'd told her we were going there, she'd have quit the show flat, no matter how much she needed the dough."

Someone had turned on all the lights for me. I got excited and I got scared.

"Hey, shamus. What's going on?"

"I'm not altogether sure, buddy." I paused. "What'd you think of her?"

"Kerry? She was broke and down and out when she got the part, but I always figured her for class. Am I right?"

"I think so. Thanks a lot."

"Shamus?"

"Yeah."

"Look out for her. She's a sweet kid."

"I'll try, and thanks again."

I slammed the phone into its cradle, grabbed my hat off the moose head and locked up shop. I pushed the elevator bell over and over. It crept up to nine and the doors opened as slowly as a bank vault's.

"Keep your shirt on, Mr. LeVine."

"I want to catch a train, Eddie."

He turned and smiled. "A hot one, eh Mr. LeVine?"

"Very hot. A blockbuster." I was showing off.

He whistled. "Christ, Mr. LeVine. Wish I could go with you, wherever it is. It have anything to do with that doll I took up last week?"

I stared at him and he knew he'd hit the jackpot. Eddie smiled all over.

"Maybe I will take you into the business, Eddie. You've got the nose."

The elevator stopped. "Main floor, Mr. LeVine. First case I take, she's gotta have big knockers."

"All my cases have big knockers, Eddie." LeVine the big shot idol of office boys and messengers. But I was working up a fine head of excitement; this bewildering ball-breaker of a case was becoming comprehensible.

It was still an hour before the lunch traffic, so I grabbed

a hack with no trouble and got to Penn Station in five minutes. Cabbie #5322–106–8632, Lou LaMonte, admirably filled the time, first by whistling "Lazy Mary, Will You Get Up?" and then by telling me about two Negroes he'd picked up the night before.

"This one shine had a diamond ring the size of an apple." He turned around. "Swear to Christ, this big." He made a circle with his thumb and middle finger and sailed through a red light.

"You ran the light, Lou."

"Fuck the lights."

I liked his style, threw him a bill for the fifty-cent ride and ran into big Penn. I knew the schedules cold, raced to Gate 26 and had the 11:40 to Philly, Baltimore, and Washington beat by five minutes. The train was crowded: half soldiers and half businessmen and I could only manage a seat next to a chubby Rotarian. We were right across the aisle from the john and the traffic was murder.

The Rotarian was red-faced Fred Garnett, whose card said "Notions, Dry Goods." While I was trying to piece together this incredible jigsaw of the Kerry Lane affair, the train started forward with that inevitably surprising and jarring first tug, and Fred was babbling on about the notions business.

"Now your products for the home, that's where your money is once this war is over."

I grunted. Kerry blackmailed, Fenton-Rubine killed, by whom?

"Course, if I had any loose change I'd get into home-building faster'n you could say Jack Robinson. This whole prefabrication process is going to pick up steam in about, say, five years. Put together houses easy as a model train set, probably easier." He chuckled. "Then you've got yourself a multi-*billion*-dollar business."

I had to get rid of him. Some people might let you alone, but not the Freddie Old Boy Garnetts of the world.

"Didn't get your line, mister," he said.

"Government work," I said stonily.

"Uh, huh." He chuckled. "That's the life. Get a civil service job and never let go."

I said nothing. His smile drooped a little around the edges. "Civil service?"

"Hardly," I said, giving him a truly evil smile. "And I really would rather not talk about it here, Fred, if you don't mind." I whipped out an old customs inspector badge someone once gave me for a gag. Before he could read the fine print, it was tucked inside my jacket again.

"Spy stuff, huh," he said.

I gave him a long hard stare. It's not my best weapon and you have to be pretty dumb to take it seriously. Fred did.

"I'm sorry," he mumbled. He went back to his little manila folder and I tried to do some more thinking. I wasn't used to complicated cases and I had to take this one from the top: Kerry scared, visits LeVine, says she's being blackmailed by someone named Fenton. Dirty films. Butler finds out, she's out of show. Visit Fenton, Fenton dead. Call from Butler. Being blackmailed, girl in show, doesn't want publicity. Go to Smithtown, nobody home. Call Butler, Butler upset. Picture of Dewey and banker, newspapers all over. Visit from Rubine. Rubine scared, Rubine dead. Threats to LeVine, threats to Butler. By whom? For what reason? Kerry gone someplace, maybe Philadelphia. I was hitting Philly almost blind, but I was curiously optimistic. Also I was talking to myself. Fred was listening. I turned on him and he bounded out of his seat like a man with a hotfoot.

"'Scuse me. Guess I'm just an old busybody," he said, smiling miserably. He pushed open the air-locked door and hurried to the next car. A very young soldier observed the scene and smiled at me. I nodded gravely but he just laughed. His leg was in a cast and he was home and things that went on in Pennsy cars were pretty small and comic to him. He was right, but I had my little work to do. Like think of a way to gain access to the inner sanctum of a banker named Eli W. Savage. You remember him. The guy shaking hands with Tom Dewey.

The train crawled into Thirtieth Street Station for about twenty minutes: stopping, starting, stopping again. The soldiers cursed loudly and I cursed softly. It was nearly two o'clock and I took the expression "banker's hours" seriously. Savage might be on the golf course already. We did the last three hundred feet into the station at a maddening pace, with everyone up and shoving their way down the aisles. The train finally wheezed to a stop and the bodies, mainly the ones in khaki, flew out the doors like paper streamers. I got jammed up behind a man in a green suit who was trying to pull his suitcase off the rack. The delay fouled me up good; by the time I reached the bank of phones inside the terminal, all were in use, and dozens of people milled outside the booths. I beat it out of the station and found a greasy spoon across the street. It was small and had a dull gray sign that said: EAT. I opened the door and got a funny kind of look from the gray-haired counterman. I was the only white man in there.

"Phone?"

"Right in back of you, mister."

"It work?" I asked stupidly. The counterman grunted and turned back to his grill, more interested in the hamburger patties than a guy who couldn't quite believe that the phone in a colored joint might work. I elbowed past a couple of tall brown men who were wearing the speckled white overalls and white caps of house painters, and got to the phone. It was an old-fashioned number with the mouthpiece mounted on the trunk and the ear piece separate. Looked like the original.

I took out my wallet and removed the clipping of Dewey and Savage. Quaker National Bank prexy, it said. Information gave me the bank's number. I dialed and asked for Mr. Savage.

"Which one, sir?" asked the middle-aged female voice at the other end.

"Number one. Eli W. himself."

"Eli Junior or Eli Senior?"

"How old is Junior?"

"Oh, Junior must be around thirty-five by now," she told me. It was like chatting around a pot-bellied stove.

"Then give me Senior."

"I'll ring it for you. Good luck."

From the folksy, talkative, and democratic lady down at the main switchboard, I was thrust miles up the social ladder, past all the ordinary Joes and Janes who spent their lives doing Quaker National's arithmetic, past all the unctuous loan officers and nervous vice-presidents, up through all the wires to that domain where the air is thin and executives speak in assured and pear-shaped tones. I got Savage's secretary. If the switchboard lady was the general store, then Savage's secretary was the Ritz.

"President Savage" was all she said.

I played it for laughs. "Could I speak with him please?"

"Excuse me?"

"President Savage. I'd like to speak with him."

"You see Sugar Ray last night?"

"He boxed the man outta the *ring*."

I stuck a finger in my ear. Maybe this wasn't the best place to call from. I felt a tap on my shoulder. A stocky Negro in a cream-colored suit and a red shirt smiled at me and pointed at the phone. I pulled the finger out of my ear and held it up, gesturing "one minute." He smiled again and turned back to the counter.

"Sir, are you still on?" came the voice.

"Yes, can President Savage be spoken with?"

"May I have your name and business."

"I'm Jack LeVine, the private investigator, and I must see President Savage in connection with some personal matters of concern to him."

"I see." She didn't. "I'll connect you with President Savage's private secretary. Hold on, please."

"I'm calling from a . . ." but I was marooned on "hold." There was another tap on my shoulder. His smile was less sincere this time. So was mine.

"Hello," came a frosty female voice.

I tried again. "I'm Jack LeVine, a private investigator from New York, and I've come to Philadelphia to speak with President Savage regarding a personal matter."

She didn't sound too impressed. "Roughly what does this personal matter concern, Mr. LeVine? I'm the president's private secretary and I assure you I have his confidence. In what area, roughly, does your inquiry fall?"

I leaned back and threw the high, hard one, letter high. "It concerns President Savage's daughter."

Her voice froze up solid—it could have split the *Titanic*. "I cannot imagine what you are talking about, sir. Good afternoon."

I listened to the hum at the other end. I looked at the ear piece and felt the warm breath of Red Shirt in back of me. I handed him the ear piece. "It's all yours."

"Sound like someone give you the shuffle." His voice was rich and mellow, like a radio announcer's. The bass notes hung in the air.

"Everybody gives me the shuffle."

He laughed heartily and shook his head, then called to the counterman.

"Hey George. Everybody givin' this fay the shuffle. Why don't you feed him?"

I realized I was pretty hungry, so I asked Red Shirt what I should get.

"Hi, sweetie," he said into the phone. "No, I'm at George's. Hold on." He smiled at me. "George makes the best fried egg sandwich in Philly."

I ordered one. George made the best fried egg sandwich in Philly or anywhere else. I don't know what he spiced it with, but it was a genuine fire-eating sensation. Belching happily, I lurched out into the street. My breath was so foul I couldn't have gotten in to see a newsboy on his day off, much less Savage.

So I went over to the Quaker National Bank.

Quaker national's main office was a predictable fifteen-story limestone affair on Chestnut Street. It was pretty clear that I'd never get in to see Savage unless everything fell into place in a big hurry. The best I could do was stay in the general area until it did. I stood around the marble lobby for a while, buying some gum and reading the *Inquirer,* but a security guard started looking at me like I was the guy who chucked the Haymarket Square bomb. When he went over to talk to another guard, I figured it was time to get out of the lobby. I either had to blow, ride the elevators up and down, or see if I could crash the fifteenth floor, where the Quaker big domes had their lair. There was only one way I could stay on fifteen for more than two minutes without getting bounced and it involved a ploy so transparent and juvenile that it positively embarrassed me. I decided to try it.

The ploy required breeziness and assurance, so I loosened my tie and let the sweat trickle from my hat without bothering to mop it. As the doors parted on fifteen, I pasted on the famous humble grin and confronted a steely brunette who sat behind the reception desk. I strode out of the elevator, jaunty and composed, my hat thrust back on my head. The rugs were so thick I felt I was on a pogo stick and the reception area was Goy Traditional, all browns and grays, walnut, hunting scenes, and discreet lighting. The room was of a modest size, nothing like the upholstered parking lot Butler called an office.

The brunette looked at me alertly. Hanging behind her was an oil of Eli W. Savage, arms crossed, red drapery. He stared straight at you, his hair combed out in little eagle's wings over the temples. There was a Latin inscription on the frame. Translated, it meant: Your Payment Is Overdue.

"Can I help you?" the brunette asked. Her expression said, "Either you're delivering a package or you're on the wrong floor."

"Building inspection, m'am." I flashed an old inspector's card and hoped for the best. The card has been mine since a bleak and windswept day in 1942 when I encountered a dead building inspector on a rooftop in Williamsburg. His death wasn't so surprising, since he had been trying to play cute with some very unpleasant people, and I pocketed his card with a great lack of emotion. I've had it ever since, and use it maybe twice a year. Lawrence D'Antonio, #3674.

"What do you have to inspect?"

"Routine check: fire, structural weakness, sanitary conditions. Nothing to worry about."

"I meant what offices in particular?"

"All of them. I'll bet it's been a long time since the president of the bank had his office looked at." With my luck it was yesterday, but the brunette appeared thrown for a small loss and I breathed a little easier. She smiled.

"You know, I suppose you're right. Could you wait a minute?" She picked up her phone and dialed three digits. There was a pause and then some dull squawking over the wire.

"Madge, I've got a building inspector out here. We haven't had an inspection yet this year, have we?" She listened for a second, then looked up at me. "You have an appointment?"

I laughed. Mr. Civil Service, taking a little pad out of his pocket.

"Not allowed to let you know in advance. That's the law, m'am. I'm sorry. Oh, excuse me." I took off my hat. Maybe I was overdoing it, but the brunette seemed to be swallowing it in chunks.

She spoke into the phone. "He says they're not allowed to make appointments. It's the law."

I looked around the room, nodding my head, impressed.

The brunette looked up and asked me to sit down. "President Savage's secretary will be out in a moment. You've caught us quite by surprise."

"We always do." I chuckled and took a seat in an over-stuffed red leather chair. The elevator doors opened and two gray-haired men emerged. I checked the painting: neither of them was Savage. The brunette greeted them: "Mr. Miller, Mr. Sampson." They looked at me, saw that I was nobody and turned away, veering off to the right.

"Is the president in yet, Kay?" asked Miller.

"He had lunch in his office, Mr. Miller, and he doesn't wish to be disturbed for the rest of the afternoon."

"I see." Miller looked sad. Sampson looked happy that Miller looked sad. Swell guys. I crossed my legs and wondered why Savage wasn't leaving his office today. Heckle and Jeckle went off to their carpeted cages as a door opened on the left and a stern fiftyish number with blue hair and a tweed suit walked out.

"Madge Durham is the president's private secretary," said the brunette. "Madge, this is Mr. . . ."

"D'Antonio." I flashed the card again. "This shouldn't take very long."

"You're quite sure you couldn't come back tomorrow, Mr. D'Antonio?" Miss Durham asked. She had on fake pearls and her glasses hung around her neck by a cord.

"I'm sorry, but it's the law, like I said before."

"Well, I suppose the law shall be served," she said, trying to look comfortable and failing miserably. "But *must* you inspect President Savage's inner office today? He's been in an extremely important meeting all day and, really," she checked her watch, "it should continue for another few hours."

I smiled. "Mr. Savage is an extremely important member of the community, Miss Durham. I'll see what I can do."

She practically fainted with relief. "That would be very much appreciated." This was very, very nice. Miss Durham pushed the door open and then another door and I was in a long carpeted corridor. Seascapes lined the walls. I gawked obviously enough for Miss Durham to notice.

"The president picked these all out himself. He's quite a collector."

"Yes," I said, "and quite a giver. Friends of mine in the Republican Party speak so very highly of him."

"You're a *Republican?*" she crooned.

"Sure. We'd be lost without Mr. Savage here in Philly."

"Not just in Philadelphia, I can assure you," she assured me. We went through a large outer office with floor-to-ceiling windows that overlooked downtown Philly. Three secretaries sat mutely behind their desks, dictaphone plugs stuck in their ears, their fingers rapidly skimming their typewriters. One was a tootsie deluxe: a blonde whose open suit jacket revealed a tight blue sweater that was being stretched to its limits. Maybe old Eli himself was grooming her for the presidential sack. She looked at me and wet her lips. I suppressed a soft moan. The other two women were pieces of dried fruit with beady little eyes that stayed fixed upon the keyboards.

"This is my office," Miss Durham said proudly as we came to a small room with a frosted-glass door marked "Private."

"Fine," I said, whipping out the little notebook. "I'll start in the outer corridor. There are fire escapes here, of course."

She lost a little of her color again. "Fire escapes. I can assure you they are all quite adequate."

"M'am," I said politely.

"Yes, of course. I'm sorry." Miss Durham bit her thin lip so hard it turned white under her teeth. "There's one on the other side that runs outside the offices of Mr. Miller and Mr. Davies. Over here you follow the outside corridor all the way to a window marked: 'Emergency exit.' There's a fire escape that runs along the west side of the building and runs past . . ." she could just nod her head.

"Past the president's office?"

"Yes."

"Fine." I shut the notebook. "I'll do my work and let you get back to yours. Thanks so much."

I left her office, winked at the blonde and walked to the outer corridor, then turned so I could see into Miss Durham's office again. A door at the rear of her office was closing and I could see a flash of heel as she ran down the private corridor to her chief's office. She was a hell of a secretary.

Since I couldn't dash out to Savage's fire escape without maybe someone wanting to take another look at my credentials, I had to do twenty minutes of inspectorial pantomime. I tapped walls, took fibers off rugs and chairs and put them into a little envelope, went into the executive crapper and flushed, crawled around on my knees, and was in every way the dutiful, buglike man from downtown. No one spoke to me, except Miss Durham, who offered a cup of coffee, hovered nervously for a few minutes, and then faded away.

I knocked on Miller's office and was permitted to bounce around on his fire escape, then I hit my knees again and looked over some wiring. Five minutes of that and I returned to the reception area, to examine the fire hose and take copious notes. Inventing functions for myself while appearing to follow a routine list of checks and double checks began to become very disorienting so I went out to the stairwell, locked the fire door, and killed five minutes sitting on the stairs. I emerged jotting down some more notes and began the long walk to the fire escape, the presidential fire escape.

Which is where all the fun began.

Happily, I could get to the escape without directly passing the nervous glance of Miss Durham; if she followed me out there, the whole deal was queered. But the outer corridor ran past the large outer office and then took a right angle which brought it parallel to the west wall of Savage's office. Miss Durham's office was in the rear left of the outer office, with her private corridor running west to the president's office. She couldn't see me unless she meant to; as I stepped quickly past the outer office, her door was closed.

The long corridor, like she said, ended up at a window with a red light over it and a rusted sign that said "Emergency Fire Exit Only." The window was pebbled and faced a rear courtyard, so no light was refracted, only grayness. I pushed at it and the window slid easily upward, almost too easily, as if the runners had been freshly oiled. I leaned out and immediately caught a huge cinder, the size of a snowflake, in my left eye. Dabbing at the eye with a handkerchief, I swung my right foot over the ledge, sat straddled, then turned facing the window from the outside and pulled my left foot over. The window slid shut and LeVine was on the presidential fire escape, forty feet from Savage's window.

I was now at the back of the Quaker National Building, all grimy exposed brick. There was that hollow roar you get in the courtyards of office buildings: a dull din and vibration of ventilation, updraft, and late afternoon traffic hum. Plus the inevitable smell of coffee-shop grease: this afternoon's hamburgers and fries wallowing in this morning's fat. I found myself gagging, getting the backwash of that fried egg sandwich supreme, and tried to concentrate hard on the role of building inspector. I took out a little file and chipped away at some rust, then stood up to test the weight by sort of jumping up and down without leaving my feet, like a fat man having a tantrum. The metal rattled a bit and I broke out in a cold sweat before taking out my little book and jotting down some notes like: "FE, test weight. OK." Whoever might be watching would be convinced and impressed. Correction: *was* convinced and impressed. Impressed enough to try and kill me.

Don't ask me who it was—I've never met the guy—but someone was paying him royally to develop a strong distaste for me. I had just turned aside when the first explosion of gunfire did a fine job on some brick two inches to my left—

approximately the spot where my generous and forgiving heart had been patiently beating a split second before. Right off, I figured the guy was trying to get my attention. To signal him that he had it, I hit the floor, in this case rusted metal slats which scraped my knuckles raw and jarred my bones to a fine powder. A second and third shot ripped into the brick a foot over my head. I stood up, ran two feet and crashed to the floor again, shaking the whole fire escape, as a fourth shot missed by so little as to put a buzz in my ear that stayed there a week. I was a sitting duck, crawling desperately toward Savage's window. He must've heard all this by now. The shots echoed cavernously off the three walls of the courtyard and I could hear the first confused shouts of bored office workers suddenly slammed awake. I lay still for a second, then leaped wildly forward—a bald Jewish bullfrog—as a shot flew over my ankles and creased some more brick. Three feet from Savage's window, I saw the great man himself for the first time, a gray eminence, alert and startled, looking out the window, absolutely fearless. He was opening the window as I bellowed, "Watch out," and a sixth shot shattered the top pane, missing the banker. I dove through the open half and landed on top of Savage, sending both of us to the floor.

"Who the hell are you?" he grunted.

"Stay down," I said. "There's a sniper out there." Our hearts were beating together like conga drums; under other circumstances, it might have been romantic. I heard the first sirens, then another shot ripped through Savage's window, spraying us with fragments of glass.

"Jesus Christ Almighty," Savage roared. He was very angry and goddamn impressive sounding. We lay waiting, breathing hard, and he finally said, "Please get off me," so I rolled over.

Which is when I first noticed Kerry Lane.

She was cowering behind a couch when she recognized me and gasped. I just had to smile. At least I wasn't getting shot at for a bum hunch.

"Hi, Kerry."

She smiled wanly. "You found me."

Savage looked incredulously from me to Kerry. "Anne, you know this man?"

She came crawling out from under the couch as the door flew open and Madge Durham came bursting in.

"There were shots. . . Oh my God!" She saw broken glass and three people on the floor. "Are you all right, Mr. President?"

"Yes, yes," Savage said testily, dusting off his pants. "Madge, get those curtains shut and watch yourself. Stay out of window range."

"We're probably all right now," I said.

Madge tiptoed around and pushed a button on Savage's desk. The curtains silently came together.

"Should I call the police?" she asked. Savage looked at me and I shook my head no.

"No, Madge. Get maintenance to replace those panes immediately. If the police ask for me, tell them it's absolutely impossible today. Perhaps tomorrow." He looked at me. I smiled and nodded. We were in business.

Madge looked at me. "You're not a building inspector."

"That's right." She looked desolate.

"Madge," Savage said slowly and evenly, each syllable rounded by a lifetime of giving orders, "you must speak to no one of this. And the panes must be replaced in the next five minutes. This is of the highest urgency."

"Yes, sir," she nodded and left.

Savage got up and went to the couch, sitting down on it heavily. The girl I knew as Kerry got up and sat beside him. I wanted a little distance, so I took a chair across the room.

"Anne, how do you know this man?"

"He's a private investigator I hired in New York when it started."

"What does he know?" They were having a private chat. The detective as cleaning lady.

"Not much."

"Plenty," I said pleasantly.

Kerry stared at me. "Mr. LeVine, what's happened?"

"Well, as you might have guessed from my entrance, this case is pretty important to some people. But you knew that already, right?"

"All right," Savage growled, "let's cut all the crap and find out what the story is. First, I'd like to thank you for saving my life. Thank you. Second, what is your precise involvement in and knowledge of this matter? Third, what were you doing crawling around on my fire escape?"

I took a good long look at Eli Whitney Savage, a spectacular product of the good life. If the *Mayflower* slept with Mount Rushmore, Savage would have been the result. His eyes were the deep blue of a Greek sea, his hair going white over the temples but otherwise bluish-gray. His skin was flawless, never touched by a blemish; he had the nose and chin of Jack Armstrong. Beneath the three-hundred-dollar suit, monogrammed DePinna shirt, and dark blue Sulka tie, Savage's body looked taut and trim. An American beauty rose, every inch of him: stem to stern, ass to elbow. When he looked at you, it was clear that you were being measured by a banker's yardstick: was this chump good for a thousand bills at nine percent?

I breathed deeply and went into the soft-shoe.

"First off, you're welcome, but the chances are good that if I wasn't out on the escape, your life wouldn't have been in danger; not just yet, that is, if I'm figuring things right. Second, my name is Jack LeVine, born Jacob Levine on Orchard Street in 1906, and I'm a private investigator operating out of New York City. In that capacity, I was hired by your daughter. . . ." I looked at the two of them and smiled. "I'm correct? She is your daughter?"

"Yes, yes. Anne Brooke Savage," the banker said impatiently.

"Just wanted to confirm it. I was hired by your daughter

to scare off some blackmailers. She was afraid they'd blow the whistle on her to the producer of *GI Canteen*, a Mr. Warren Butler. Now, I'd guess she was afraid they'd tell you and I'd guess, furthermore, that they have. Hence her visit to Philadelphia, after a lengthy absence?"

Anne Brooke Savage, chorus girl, nodded.

"Finally, I was on the fire escape because I was unable to get in the front door. Miss Durham serves you very, very well, Mr. Savage."

He allowed himself a smile. "She's been with me for a long time. A very loyal and courageous woman."

"Aces," I agreed.

"How did you find out I was here, Mr. LeVine?" asked Kerry. Dark circles were smeared beneath her eyes. Coming home to Philly must've been murder on her.

There was a knock at the door and Savage put a finger to his lips; two maintenance men came in respectfully, carrying panes of glass. Miss Durham followed.

Savage stood up. "Let's go to the dining room. Madge, some coffee, please."

"They called," she said obliquely.

"And?" he asked.

"A man with a rifle was spotted on the roof of Prudential. He got away."

Savage looked at me, then gestured to a side door which led into a small but elegant room with a beautiful walnut table and a crystal chandelier. The four of us walked inside.

"The Ritz," I said, ever the commoner. We took seats near the end; Miss Durham walked into the adjacent kitchen.

"Anne had asked you something, LeVine," Savage said evenly.

"She asked me how I found out. It wasn't easy, it wasn't hard. It was lucky. An assistant stage manager at the Booth told me the girl had been skittish about the possibility that *GI Canteen* might play in Philadelphia. I connected that fact and her going home, wherever that might be—probably Philly, I thought—with this picture." I unfolded the news clipping and slid it across the table. "I found this in the blackmailers' hideout on Long Island. I couldn't believe that two people had gotten murdered over a simple shakedown of a chorus girl."

"Two people?" Kerry asked.

"Very early Saturday morning, a fella by the name of Al Rubine came to my apartment, very scared, and told me where the films were stashed. Not only was it a bum steer, but Rubine was dead five hours after he told me."

"Rubine?" Savage said contemplatively, asking himself a quiet question.

"You know him?" I asked.

"A man by that name, or something very close to it, contacted me about four days ago."

"In connection with the blackmail of your daughter?"

Savage looked at Anne. Anne looked at me. I looked at Savage.

"Tell him, father. He's very trustworthy . . ."

"Like your other friends, Anne?" His tone made you reach for a fur coat.

"I think we've covered all that ground, father," she said unawed. "I don't think we have to squabble in front of Mr. LeVine." Suddenly I thought of Katie Hepburn in *The Philadelphia Story*, and it all seemed very right, and I wanted things to turn out just great for Miss Anne Savage.

"Prodigal daughter," I said, the cool professional. "I see it every day. Your daughter's a fine girl, Mr. Savage, and in my business you learn to judge character. If you can't, your life expectancy tops out at about thirty-five. She got caught in a mistake, not an uncommon one for rich girls who want to experience the world a little, who get bored with having everything done for them. What's uncommon is the way she stuck up for you, protected you every step of the way, until I had to crawl around on a fire escape and take more flak than the Fifth Army to find out she was your daughter." Anne was sniffling. "You ought to be proud of Annie, Mr. Savage, very proud." Curtain. When I'm good, I'm very good.

"All right," Savage said, clearing his throat. "You are a private detective. From this moment on, consider yourself a top-secret detective. What I tell you is absolutely and strictly between you and me. If you talk in your sleep . . ."

"I get the point. You don't want me to tell anybody."

Miss Durham paraded out of the kitchen, holding a silver tray which held a silver coffeepot and exquisite china coffee cups.

"What does she know?" I asked.

"Everything," Savage said. She poured the coffee and kissed Anne's cheek, which started Anne bawling. "Mrs. Savage passed away when Anne was ten. Madge has always been like a mother to her."

"When Annie ran away," Madge started to say, before a look from the banker stopped her cold. "Excuse me." She backed out of the room.

We sipped at our coffee in silence. Anne dried her tears and forced a smile in my direction.

"It'll be okay," I said. She just nodded.

Savage wiped his mouth with a linen napkin. "I'm ready."

"So am I."

"Fine. Here's the story in a nutshell. The blackmailers used Anne to get at me. They threaten release of the films and a great embarrassment to a reputation the Savages have built in Philadelphia for two hundred years."

"Unless you pay up?"

He permitted himself a chilly little excuse for a smile. "Quite the contrary, LeVine. Unless I *don't* pay up—to the Republican Party. I've been a principal contributor to, and fund raiser for, the Dewey campaign. The convention started in Chicago this morning. I'll fly there tomorrow—that's the 27th—and we anticipate that Tom will be nominated on the first ballot Wednesday. After that we'll be on the go, fighting all the way." He punctuated the last four words by beating his fist on the table. "Three terms was bad enough; four is unthinkable. This isn't a monarchy, this is a democracy."

I looked around the private dining room. "Nice chandelier."

Savage raised a bushy eyebrow. "Look, LeVine, I don't care if you like my politics. This is just blackmail, pure and simple."

"I agree one hundred percent. To tell you the truth, I don't care for anybody's politics very much. I do my fund raising strictly for Jack LeVine, the people's choice. You back Dewey and that's jake with me. If you were a vegetarian, likewise. Pay me and I'll try and do a job."

"I like that very much." Savage was staring straight into my eyes. "I'm not asking you to love Dewey—God knows his manners could be better—but to give me some efficient detective work. If we understand that, I'm sure we'll get along fine."

"No doubt about it."

"Excellent. As for payment, I will give you a retainer of one thousand dollars, with fifteen hundred more payable upon the completion of the job."

That was nearly as much money as I'd made all last year. Bankers didn't usually come my way.

"Tell you what, Mr. Savage, I travel pretty light, so how about three hundred now and hold the other twenty-two until it's all over. Then maybe I'll take the rest of my life off."

"The fee's too large?" he asked, eyes twinkling. A little banker's humor.

"Not for this case. Your daughter gave me twenty and I almost got killed twice. The Savages owe me a little comfort."

Anne smiled. Savage smiled. I smiled. Not grins, just a bit of polite fun among three strangers stuck on a life raft.

"They set any deadline for a decision, Mr. Savage?"

"Two weeks."

"That's not so bad. It gives me a little leeway to operate.

I only have one question: what the hell do you want me to do?"

"Get the films," Anne said.

"Perhaps," Savage said, "if that's possible. Mainly, I wish to avoid embarrassment and remain an active member of Mr. Dewey's campaign. The possibility of a Cabinet post for me is not a remote one. I want to find out who's in back of this and I wish them flushed out, scared off, or whatever. I've got a hunch about this, LeVine. Dewey made plenty of enemies when he was D.A. in New York and the Syndicate knows that if he were elected, the FBI would be on their trail night and day. I'm convinced organized crime is in back of this. Obviously, I don't dare do anything by myself."

"That's very wise, Mr. Savage. But I'm not sure what I could do against the mob by myself."

"You have friends, contacts. Use them." Savage abruptly stood up. "Keep my name out of it and make it sticky for them, so sticky that they back out. Obviously, it is not a simple situation. If it were, I wouldn't be paying you twenty-five hundred dollars to clear it up." He extended his hand. "Now good luck, I think you'd better get started. I'll be in Chicago starting tomorrow, at the Pioneer Hotel, room 1115, through Thursday. I want daily reports."

He didn't want much for his money, only that I commit suicide and keep his name out of it. That's if his hunch was on the money. I wasn't so sure.

"If I bring this off, tell Dewey to make me head of the FBI. Hoover's getting too old for the job."

Savage was thoughtful. "You have any ideas about this?"

I said yes and went out the door.

15

ONE OF THEM looked like Tony Galento after a week-long bender; the other was just a little smaller than a two-family house. Leaning against a long black Packard on my sleepy, tree-lined block in Sunnyside, they stuck out like hard-ons in a Turkish bath. I spotted them two blocks down, while still on the "el" platform. After staring at them through my pocket binoculars, I decided that I had neither the wit nor the energy to play with them. It had been too long a day. I looked a bit more. The squat one was yawning and cracking his knuckles; the big one was picking his nose. They were drawing all kinds of funny looks from my neighbors, regular Joes coming home from work with the papers under their arms.

I went to a pay phone next to the turnstile, called the precinct house and asked for a captain who owed me a favor, a guy by the name of Joe Egan.

"Joe, there's some muscle hanging around outside my house. Be a nice lad and chase them for me."

"Muscle? Outside your place? I didn't know you were that important." Cops have to pass some kind of humor quiz before they get on the force.

"Can you hear me laughing, Joe? People tell me that sometimes it's hard to, over the phone. Listen, I don't know what these mugs want and I don't have the strength to find out, not right now."

"What kind of a case is this?" he asked in his raspy growl of a voice.

"Beats me. Nothing I'm working on right now. Frankly, I'm baffled, Joe."

"Sure you're baffled. You don't know what the hell is going on. What is it this time, Jack, hiding a witness? Working against us? You know I'd like to see you get your head broken, so you'd go back to the fur business where you belong. A Jew shamus can't cut the mustard, Jack, I've always told you that."

"You'll get rid of them, then?"

Egan sighed. "I owe you a favor and I'm one of these big-hearted Irish assholes you always read about. I'll send a couple of boys over. But if this case is anything important, I wish to hell you'd level with me."

"Don't worry about it. I don't handle important cases, they make me cry. Now give me a break and hurry it up, Joe. I want to go home."

"I'll give you a break, a break on . . ." I hung up on him. It was a private joke. I always hung up on him. He was a good boy and proved it two minutes later when a nicely polished squad car came rolling up the street. The gorillas turned around to watch it and I dashed down the stairs, ran three blocks—one east, two south, cut through Roth's hardware on Murray Street, out the back door, and into the basement entrance of my building. I took the elevator up and pushed the door open very slowly when I got to three. There was no one in the hall, no one outside my door. My door was locked. I didn't smell smoke or gas and I didn't hear screams, so I unlocked it. No one was waiting inside with a sap or a rod, no one floating in my bathtub. I was surprised. LeVine returns home after a day at the office.

Down on the street, the cops were walking away from the muscle, turning around and making with the big cop arm-waving gestures. The gorillas were laying on the wounded pride and the cops were smiling. Nobody was fooling anybody today: the cops even held the doors for the mugs when they got in their car. "Beat it, c'mon," the patrolman said simply, and the two drove off.

The sergeant looked up at my window and I recognized him as a drinking chum of Egan's. He saluted. I saluted back, fished a quarter out of my pocket and threw it down three stories. It pinged on the sidewalk. The cop laughed, but he also put the quarter in his pocket. A genuine lawman: laughing at the craziness of it all and keeping whatever he could get his mitts on.

I closed the white lace curtains, flopped on the couch, and dialed the Hotel Lava.

Dandruff answered and I asked for Toots Fellman. He was cranky about it, of course, and it took a while. Finally, a businesslike, "Fellman."

"Toots, it's LeVine."

"Jack! I've tried calling you about five times. How's that chorus girl case coming along?"

"I'm in over my head, Toots, and you're the only person I'd tell that to."

"Who's involved and how bad is it?"

"Everybody, I think, starting with Hitler and working down to Fenton. How bad? Pretty bad."

"You can't figure it?"

"I *can* figure it, that's what makes it so awful."

He laughed and laughed. Private dicks and press agents enjoy trading disasters more than they enjoy swapping triumphs. I think it has something to do with cynicism.

"You can't tell me anything, right Jack?"

"Right, but you've got to do me one more favor. If it'll queer you with anyone, forget it, but if not, I'd appreciate it."

"Cut the schmooze, Jack, what is it?"

"Shea at Homicide hates my guts and I don't want to talk to him, but I've got a hunch he might be a weather vane on this case."

"You want me to call him and test him?"

"Close, Toots, very close. Tell him LeVine thinks he has a big lead on the Fenton murder and that body they found up in Olive day before yesterday."

"I heard it was a con named Rubine."

"From who?"

"Friend of mine."

"On the inside?"

"Sort of. He said Rubine was strictly a bum, a twelve-time loser with a record full of nickel-and-dime stuff."

"He tell you anything else?"

"That was it. I pressed him a little and he made like a clam."

That made me very happy. "I'm not surprised. Tell Shea I think the two murders are connected."

"What if he wants to call you in?"

"Ten-to-one he doesn't want any part of me, Toots. If you think he might, tell me and I'll blow town for a few days."

"But you're sure he won't?"

"Positive."

"This is that big, huh?"

"Shea won't touch it with rubber gloves, mark my words."

"I'll call you back soon as I know anything."

LeVine showered. Soaping my armpits, my trademark dome, between my toes, my heels and knees, my nuts; then letting a nice warm stream wash away all the Philly fire escape dirt and all the rich odors of anxiety. The drain gurgled; the phone rang. I let it ring and it didn't quit until after twenty tries. The hell with them: it couldn't be Toots and nobody else mattered. Kitty Seymour? Probably not.

LeVine shaved, powdered, moved his bowels and read the *World-Telegram*. The Allies had cut off the Cherbourg peninsula and we were bouncing shells off the Japs' heads in Saipan. The Republican Convention had opened in Chicago. Dewey was a shoe-in: he'd fly in from Albany when he got the nod. Looked like Governor Earl Warren for veep. And Eli W. Savage for Secretary of the Treasury? The father of Anne Brooke Savage, whose rounded breasts and ginger-spice *mons* passed before the public's eye in *Hollywood Maidens* and $2 + 2 = 69$? Reading about the convention made my participation in the whole process seem even more implausible than it was. But facts were facts, and the chunky man taking a Sunnyside shit was a mover and shaker of world events.

And he didn't know the half of it.

The phone started ringing again, but I wasn't going anywhere. Major Hoople told Martha that he had been instrumental in bringing the Hun to his knees during the first war. Nobody believed him. Some kids were tying cans to a cat's tail in "Out Our Way" and Alley Oop was running around with a club in his hand. "Believe It Or Not" informed me that an Australian tribe wore live cobras as jewelry and that one Frank W. Bludgeon of Mackinac, Michigan, was born with a hand full of thumbs—"ALL THUMBS" said the headline. I chose to believe neither story. Yanks versus Browns tomorrow at the Stadium; Browns, incredibly enough, in first place by 4½ over the Yanks. Atley Donald against Bob Muncrief, and the phone was ringing again. Enough was enough.

When I picked up, I got a very official-sounding lady who asked me if I was Mr. Jack LeVine, the private investigator.

"Correct."

"Please hold for General Redlin."

General Redlin? The army General Redlin, the "Gray Eagle"? Hero of the Kuriles, all three stars worth?

"Is this a gag?" but I was speaking to the mouthpiece. Not for long.

"Hello," came a rich baritone, "this is General Redlin. Am I addressing a private investigator by the name of . . ." I could hear him shuffling through some papers, "of Jack Levine?"

"LeVine, like Hollywood and Vine. Is this really General Redlin I'm speaking to?"

"Himself. The Gray Eagle." He laughed. I liked that. "You're obviously surprised, Mr. LeVine."

"Not really. FDR told me you'd call."

"What!" The laughter drained from his voice like water from a tub. "The president has contacted you himself?"

"No, no. Calm down, general. It was just a little banter. I'm known for my light touch."

And for fainting. I sat down heavily, my ears ringing. It

was all over my head, the whole deal. Getting fired on in Philly, working for Savage, now coming home to be called by a three-star general who seriously thought I had Roosevelt on hold.

"He hasn't called, then?" Redlin still wasn't sure.

"No, general. Not yet."

"Yes." He cleared his throat. "It would be very premature for him to . . ." He trailed off. I took a potshot.

"To get involved at this level."

"Exactly. I was told you were a sharp fellow, LeVine. I can see that already."

"Yes." I trailed off this time.

"Well." There was an awkward silence. "Uhm . . . things have gotten a bit snafued on this side, LeVine, and we'd like to speak with you."

"That's fine with me. I've got a cozy little office at 1651 Broadway. Room 914. Come in anytime."

"We've got to speak with you tomorrow at 8:00 A.M., room 3521, Waldorf Towers. Breakfast will be served."

"Delightful. I like my eggs scrambled well-done, and easy with the butter on my toast."

I was treading water with the jokes, but Redlin didn't know that. He thought I was trying to be a wiseass.

"If you served under me, sir, I would have you court-martialled for insolence." His voice was very, very hard.

"Okay, the hell with it," I said, and hung up. I sat by the phone. My hands were trembling. It rang again.

"You *will* be there tomorrow?"

"What about my insolence? And why should I be there?"

"It's extremely complicated, LeVine, but we'll try and explain tomorrow. Let me just say that we feel your employ by Eli W. Savage is not in the interests of national security."

"Now I'm a traitor." It was my turn to get testy.

"No, no, certainly not," he crooned. "You'll understand after the meeting."

"Who exactly am I meeting with?"

"Top personnel, LeVine."

"What does that mean: Churchill and Stalin? Or just Eisenhower?"

"You're very flip, but I don't think you'll stay that way," he sounded more sure of himself. "Now, would you like to be picked up by limousine?"

"No. They haven't seen a limo in Sunnyside since Capone visited a speakeasy he used to own on 45th Street. My neighbors would bother me."

"We'd like to be certain that you'll be there."

"I wouldn't miss this for the world, general. Now why don't you tell me who's going to be there?"

"The front pages will be there, Mr. LeVine."

"I'm used to the funny pages, but maybe it's the same thing. I'd sure love to meet Moon Mullins, though."

He laughed again, this three-star general. "So would I, LeVine. So would I." He waited for me to say something else. I didn't. He cleared his throat, said, "Fine, then," for no reason at all and hung up.

I mixed a very fat drink and then another and was half in the bag when Toots called back. By this time, what he had to say was superfluous. Of course, Shea told him that he was off the case. Toots asked why and was told to go take a walk, who was he to bother Homicide with questions, did he want to lose his license, et cetera?

"When was the last time Shea was pulled off a case, Jack?"

"McKinley's assassination, I think. It's too big for him, Toots. They'd pull the Shadow, Mister Keen, and Boston Blackie off this one."

"I won't ask why."

"Go ahead and ask. I'll answer you next year. Right now it's all I can do to keep from finishing off a fifth of Johnnie Walker."

He just whistled. "I look through keyholes and the best I ever got was a vice-president of Corning getting his glass blown by a two-dollar blonde, knees down."

"I don't know what hit me, Toots. I could go for some keyhole stuff; it's easier on the nerves. And look, thanks for playing it straight with me."

"Maybe I like you, Jack."

"Yes, but do you love me?"

He laughed and I laughed, a couple of nice little guys. When I got off the phone, I was giddy and scared.

The fact was I couldn't wait for 8:00 A.M. at the Waldorf Towers.

YOU'VE NEVER BEEN THERE and you haven't missed anything. The Waldorf Towers, not so surprisingly, is just a lot of chandeliers, crystal, and ass-kissing by monkeys in red jackets; just a lucky break away from toasting frankfurter buns at Nedick's. The brass and silver is highly polished and so are the manners —if you're rich. Some of the worst people in the world stay there. They get treated very well.

Unless you have an appointment with the Allied High Command, it's hardly worth the trip.

After a restless night of thin sleep broken by tense gray periods of waking—pawing at the alarm clock, wrapping the sheets around my aching legs—I called it quits at five-thirty and brewed enough coffee to keep Luxembourg awake for a week. I was out of the house at six-thirty, like the other men and women of the day shift. I saw them drifting toward the "el" station, in ones and twos, off to the factory districts of Long Island City and Astoria. There was a light drizzle, a rain so light it hardly seemed to fall.

I walked for fifteen minutes or so, nodding at storekeepers I knew, as they swept sidewalks and unloaded cartons from trucks. I walked until some of the knots were out of my guts and then took the slow way into Manhattan, a number eleven bus that goes over the bridge to East 59th Street after winding around Sunnyside and Long Island City, stopping every other block and missing all the lights. I sat in the back and looked out the window, fiddling with my tie and brushing lint off my brown summer suit. The city looked tired and tense. Maybe it was me.

The bus finished its run at East 59th Street. It was a quarter to eight. I hoofed it over to Park and 50th in ten minutes and noticed an armada of limos double-parked outside the Towers. I leaned against one of them and lit up a Lucky and finally got up the nerve to walk inside. Once inside, the tension was thick enough to eat. Uniformed military aides and plainclothesmen were all over the place. They started eyeing me and eyeing each other, until a Waldorf minor domo came scurrying across the huge oriental carpet to ask if he could be of any help.

"I have a tryst with Omar Bradley."

He smiled a little. The domo was about 5'8" and a muscle-bound 180. Not even the little mustache could cover up the fact that he was a bouncer.

"May I be of service or I'll have to . . ."

"You're not asking me to leave, because I'm supposed to get a free plate of scrambled eggs up in 3521."

He whipped a list out of an inside jacket pocket.

"Your name please? And rank, if any?"

"Jack LeVine. Rank: second-generation American citizen."

He scanned the list and nodded.

"I'm entitled to the eggs?"

He just clapped his hands and two burly plainclothesmen came over and flanked me.

"Take him up, please," said the minor domo, and walked away. One of the plainclothes guys grunted "okay" and pointed to a waiting elevator car. I strode across the lobby, as the two men fell into step behind me and followed me into the elevator. They nodded to the jockey, a short man with a two-dollar toupee and a great sense of importance. He slammed the doors shut as crisply as a Prussian stationmaster and took us on an ear-popping flight up to thirty-five. There he rocketed the doors open, stepped aside and bowed. The plainclothesmen gestured for me to get out first—nobody was actually speaking —and I padded up the silent corridor wondering if maybe a lot of people had died and I was now the President of the United States.

As we reached 3521, the taller plainclothesman, a swarthy

guy with two inches on me, picked up his stride and took me under the arm, while the other stepped ahead and knocked on the door three times: knock, pause, knock-knock. The door flew open instantly and I was practically carried into a small sitting room. A wiry man in a uniform that had three stars on it bounded from his chair as I entered. A colored guy closed the door in back of me and the plainclothesmen melted into the corridor.

"Mr. LeVine, I'm General Redlin," said the wiry man. "It's a pleasure to meet you."

I nodded and shook his hand dumbly, all out of smart things to say. It was going way too fast, and maybe everybody —Kerry/Anne, Butler, Savage, this general—maybe they had me confused with some LeVine who really made things happen: a macher, a doer. I followed people around for a living, I looked for used condoms in the trash. What the hell did they want from me?

"Let's go inside," Redlin said. The Negro stepped across the room and stood by another door. He nodded inquisitively at Redlin, who did the same to me.

"Ready, Mr. LeVine?"

"Fine with me," I croaked, my voice filtered through sandpaper, cheesecloth, and broken glass. My heart was pounding so hard and so fast that I was sure Redlin could hear it. He smiled knowingly, like he had this smartass dick figured right: all bluff on the phone and jelly at the Waldorf. So I got a little boiled about that, which helped when the door was opened and I walked into a living room full of hard-looking big shots in uniform. They were already eating breakfast around a huge circular table, as men in white jackets flitted about with trays and platters.

Navy uniforms, army uniforms, RAF uniforms. Blues, whites, and greens: everything starched and stiff and clean. Manicured hands precisely carved pieces of melon. Sunburned faces were stuffed with eggs and toast. Modulated voices, used to command, whispered, buzzed, but rarely rose. Silverware clattered against plates. The waiters were silent and watched, watched, in turn, by a nervous hotel exec who snapped his fingers, pointed and raised his eyebrows to set his staff in motion. Every sound and motion stopped when I entered with Redlin. The men in uniform stopped talking and chewing; the waiters, as attuned as bats to the frequencies in the air, waited.

"Gentlemen," Redlin said, holding out his arm like an emcee, "may I have the pleasure of introducing Mr. Jack LeVine, private detective extraordinary."

I bowed and some of the men smiled, amused or intrigued. Most of them did not smile. Redlin went around the room: General This, Colonel That, Admiral Whosis, Brigadier General Whatsis. I recognized a lot of them: nobody up there with Ike, Mac, Bradley, Halsy, or Nimitz, but a good sampling of army and navy brass was in attendance; people whom I read about every day, men I genuinely admired for the job they had done in taking the Axis to the cleaners. I hadn't heard of the British colonel or the frog admiral, so I figured they might be in Intelligence.

Two of the men were civilians and they were both easily recognizable. One was Lee Factor, a political hatchet man for FDR. Factor was a gnome of a man, all tangled black hair and fleshy nose and deep-socketed eyes that brimmed over with intelligence and cunning. He would light your cigarette while the firing squad took aim.

The other man in mufti wasn't very cunning at all. In fact, when Redlin introduced us, I laughed out loud.

"I believe you know Warren Butler" was the way Redlin put it. I roared and Butler turned as red as a bowl of borscht, which made me laugh all the harder. The miserable pretentious son of a bitch. Seeing him in such blatant discomfort made me feel good all over.

Still chortling in the nastiest way I knew possible, I took a seat next to Redlin, told the white jacket that I wanted the eggs scrambled well-done, and stuck a serrated spoon into a nice piece of honeydew. Nobody else was eating. They all watched me, taking my measure. I expected it, but I didn't like it.

"Surprised that I eat with a spoon?" I asked no one in particular. The silence in the room was swallowed by an even larger silence.

"Jack, we mean you no harm," said Redlin.

"Fine," I answered. "You just wanted to throw me a free breakfast. I appreciate it." Somebody coughed. It takes a while to get used to my sense of humor.

"Shall we get down to brass tacks immediately? I feel the usual civilities bore you." Redlin's voice was getting a little frosty.

"Remind me to tell you of some civilities I got on a fire escape yesterday," I said, my mouth half-filled with melon. "You'll enjoy it."

"Ken, let's just lay it on the line with him," said a large snowy-haired admiral.

"Please do," I said.

"All right," Redlin began, "it's very simple. You have, in the past few weeks, gotten involved in matters affecting national security and we'd like you to get out before you get hurt. That's all of it."

"I don't know what you're talking about. I'm a small-time detective. There must have been a mix-up."

Lee Factor smiled.

"LeVine, I think I like you. Your innocent guile is refreshing."

"Most people make that observation," I told him. Factor laughed. I joined him. That made two people laughing.

But Factor stopped abruptly. "So why don't you stop putting on a show," he barked, running a delicate hand through his untamed hair.

"Level with me and I will."

"We want, we *urge*, you to stop working for Eli W. Savage," said General Redlin.

"Meaning what, and why?"

A rotund admiral got incensed. His name was Thomas, or Thompson. I forget.

"Who are you to insult the rank of these officers? You've been given an order by the highest military men in the country, men whose job it is to win a war. Who the hell are you to talk back to us? Get off the case and stop asking questions." A half-dozen officers murmured assent. One of the limeys said, "Quite right."

I was unawed, maybe because the admiral was the kind of bluff artist I run into all the time.

"I'm very sorry, sir, but I start asking questions when strangers start shooting at me. Maybe you military men take it for granted, but I like to know why people want to kill me."

"It's a delicate matter and things happened," said Redlin. That was his way of explaining things.

I took a look at Butler, who turned away, and then stood up, giddy with chutzpah.

"If no one wants to tell me anything, I'm getting the hell out of here." I threw down my napkin. "We're sitting around playing footsie. I ask a question and get a tap dance in return. Maybe you figured the sight of all these ribbons was going to bring me to my knees. As far as I'm concerned, that's a misuse of your power. Something goddamn ugly is going around, and all this shadowboxing isn't going to put me off. Two people have died in the past week and yesterday I was almost number three. Either you tell me what's coming off or I'm walking out of here and finding out for myself, let the chips fall wherever they damn please."

"Please sit down, LeVine," said Factor. He looked at the others. Their jaws were open—that's how good I had been. "You're right. We should tell you exactly what the situation is. Then I think you'll understand the necessity of your getting off this case."

I pointed at Butler and sat down. "He screwed this

case up nice and pretty," I ranted. "In pink ribbons he screwed it up." A waiter came over with my eggs in a covered dish. He lifted the cover.

"I'm going to eat my eggs," I announced. "While eating them I expect to get told and told straight. Like I said, people have been shooting at me and I'm curious." There are times to be a crazy man and this was one of them because when you're in as deep as I was at the Waldorf, the only way you can get out with pride and skull intact is to act so loco that people will assume that you hold all the aces. In the Savage case, I probably did. Because before sticking my fork into the eggs, I looked around the table again and observed that these men were scared, very scared.

Redlin looked at a big blond officer.

"Colonel Watts, why don't you sum it all up for Mr. LeVine."

Watts cleared his throat and started speaking. His voice came out high and comical, like a silent-screen lover in his first and last talkie.

"The reelection of Franklin Roosevelt is absolutely essential to the successful conclusion of our war effort. His defeat, which this group adjudges to be a real possibility, would be calamitous not only to the efforts of our fighting forces in Europe and the Pacific, but to the shaping of the postwar world. As Wendell Willkie said just yesterday afternoon after reading the Republican platform plank on foreign policy, it is so vague that it could lead, if implemented," and here Watts put on glasses and started reading from a newspaper, "to 'no international organization and no effective force for the suppression of aggression.' End of quote." Watts looked around the table and drew nods of assent.

"Willkie really say that?" I asked.

Watts pounded the newspaper, the *Times*. "It's here in black-and-white."

Warren Butler was biting his nails. He caught me watching him and blushed.

Watts continued: "The defeat of Dewey, then, is a defense priority. We feel it necessary to cut off his principal source of revenue. Eli W. Savage figures prominently in the Dewey strategy, both as a contributor and a fund raiser. Contacts were made and Warren Butler informed Lee Factor that he was in possession of films made by Savage's daughter that were sufficiently injurious to the Savage name as to cripple his effectiveness in the campaign. Since the operation had to be carried out extragovernmentally, Warren Butler was placed in charge of the matter, reporting to Lee Factor. Coded progress memos were to be filed weekly."

I smiled at Butler. He was scared shitless and knew that I knew it.

"So Butler hired me as a blind," I said through a mouthful of bacon.

"Correct," said Redlin.

"Now what?" I asked.

"Now," the general said, "we hope you see our position and get off the case."

"And if I say no?"

"We hope you say yes. It wouldn't do you very much good to say no."

I smiled broadly. It wasn't a very nice smile. "It wouldn't do you gentlemen very much good if anybody found out how this deal was totally mishandled, would it?" I asked coyly. "Does the whole military know about this? Are your careers on the line for you to go to such extremes in support of FDR? Or did Mr. Factor just snow you into thinking so?" I looked at Factor. He looked at his sleeve. "General Redlin, is the entire military hierarchy in back of this? I could find out very easily. Couple of phone calls . . ."

Redlin flushed. "What good would it do you to find out?"

"Maybe a great deal. Look, maybe I'll help you gentlemen out and maybe I won't, but the way I figure it, you don't have me over any kind of a barrel. It wouldn't be very hard to lock me up under some pretense, but I'd bet that your last hope is that I'm Mr. Nice Guy and keep my mouth shut about this botch."

"Botch?" Factor asked innocently.

"Of course it's a botch. It's a scandal. Not only is it blackmail, but crude blackmail. You let this clown of a producer play gangbusters, and he goes out and hires fourth-rate palookas like Fenton and Rubine, who couldn't stick up a candy store without shooting themselves in the asshole. If this is high-level blackmail, then I'm Walter Winchell. This has been a nickel-dime operation from start to finish: the federal government going out to hire cheap gunsills and not even paying them enough to keep them loyal."

"Shut up!" Butler bellowed, the veins bulging out of his neck. "Shut up, you bastard!"

"You have two murders on your head, Broadway," I told him. "You'll have to be more polite than that if you want me to keep it quiet. You hire mugs for two bits, then get surprised when they get a whiff of the real gravy and try to put the squeeze on you. So you have to kill one and then the other. No wonder you were shocked when I told you Rubine had blown Smithtown. He knew you had fingered Fenton for trying to shake you down and he knew he was next. So instead of a simple, if high-stakes, blackmail deal you have two dead crooks and a stink so bad you have to call in the army and navy to bail you out. You try bumping me off and screw that up. And here I am, still alive but very angry and with the strong suspicion that you folks are in big trouble. FDR isn't going to like hearing about this, is he, Factor?"

Factor shook his head. "Just help us out, LeVine. You're right. We need you. Please help us."

"I might have at the beginning, but not now. The best I'll do is try and keep your names out of it—if you lay off my client. But if you think I'm going to roll over and play dead while you blackmail Savage and his daughter, you're crazy. I don't like Dewey, but I don't like extortion either. My politics are strictly for LeVine. I don't care if Attila the Hun wins this November."

I got up and walked toward the door. A few mouths were open and all eyes were on me. I'm no megalomaniac, but at this moment I felt clearly superior to every other living creature.

"If you have plans to bump me off, forget it. It doesn't worry me and it wouldn't help you even if you managed to do it right. Other people are on to this mess." I stared at Butler. "This thing has been blown so bad my Aunt Sylvia could find out what happened. In fact, I'm your only chance. Savage trusts me."

"Savage must not be a contributor to this campaign," Redlin said, his voice shaking.

"You're whistling in the dark, all of you. If you had any brains you would have let me handle this from the beginning." I was heading down the stretch, ears pricking in the breeze. "Savage would be on a slow boat to Tierra del Fuego by now."

The Negro opened the door for me. I started out, then turned back to the group. They appeared paralyzed.

"And I would have done it cheap."

I winked at the guy holding the door. He didn't laugh, but his eyes did. Then he closed the door.

"Rough crowd," I said.

"Yessir." He paused. "They had you figured for a chump. I heard 'em."

"Everybody does."

"You're no chump, Mister."

"Keep it under your hat."

The door opened behind me. Factor, Butler, Redlin, and Colonel Watts came out. I pointed at Butler.

"Get him the hell out of my sight."

"Jack," Warren Butler said. "Jack." He was lost. Factor whispered to him and he forlornly returned to the other room.

"LeVine, you're being very, very rash," said Factor. "You could get hurt."

"I'm sick and tired of being threatened. It's a bore."

"I figured you for a man who loved his country," Redlin blushed almost as he said it. It was too nauseating even for him.

"That's priceless, general, really. You love your country so much you can put the squeeze on a twenty-year-old girl for making a not-very-terrible mistake, and you can stick some schlemiel of a crook head first into a drainpipe. If that's patriotism then I'm Tokyo Rose."

"It has been unpleasant and terrible, LeVine. Granted." Redlin was cranking out the sincerity now, having tried everything else. "I've been appalled again and again at the manner in which this operation has been executed. If we had fought the war this way, the Germans would be in Ohio by now. But," and he took a deep, sincere breath, "what's done is done, and this operation must be seen through to its conclusion. Please help us. If you'd like, it could be made very profitable for you." And now, finally, he had tried to buy me. Redlin looked at Factor, who waved his sculptor's fingers.

"Take that for granted, LeVine," said Factor.

"No dice. I won't make it worse for you, that's my side of the bargain. Your side is stopping all the muscle. If you sic anyone on me, I'll sing so sweetly you'd think I was Russ Colombo. You understand that? The election's four and a half months off. That's a long time. If this thing breaks between now and then, Dewey could goose-step down Fifth Avenue and he'd still get elected. Play it smart and leave me alone. Ask anybody in this town: I know how to talk and I know how to keep quiet."

Redlin bit his lip and Factor shook his head. I was a nut. I left and the door closed. The two plainclothesmen were waiting outside. They rode down with me in the elevator. I thanked them and gave them my card.

17

IT WAS A MORNING to go through mail and sort things out. I had gotten a bad case of the shakes after walking out of the Waldorf and had hailed a cab to get me to the office. Being cheeky was one thing, but telling three-star generals, admirals, and FDR's top errand boy to take a jump was something out of an opium dream. I didn't have much choice, the way I figured it; I was the man in the middle, a pawn in the biggest crap game going. When I added things up, it meant I could decide the outcome of the 1944 presidential election unless I kept everybody at a stalemate. I had to keep the Democrats too scared to lean on Savage, and keep Savage in the dark as to who was behind it—or else the blackmail would get turned around. It would be my all-time juggling act, maybe anyone's all-time juggling act, and there was a good chance that all the oranges would bounce off my head. I had to hold my ground against pressures that weren't going to be pretty. If those pressures were sustained over a span of months, chances were I'd end up walking around Creedmore in a bathrobe and slippers, trying to crap on the ceiling.

So as I opened a letter from the Handwriting Institute of America, dedicated to the "scientific analysis of penmanship," I decided to get everybody off my back by mid-July. I didn't know how to do it, but just making the decision stopped my knees from knocking together. After calling Savage's Chicago hotel and leaving word that I'd be out all afternoon, I rang up Toots Fellman and made a date to spend the afternoon holding hands at the Yankee–Browns game.

Toots and I got up to the Bronx an hour or so early, to get a head start on the Ballantine and to settle back to enjoy a thoroughly ridiculous ball game. In return for his many favors,

I treated Toots to boxes in the mezzanine, along the first-base line. Very nice seats, because we could make side bets on leg hits. The guy would start down the line and Toots or I would yell "safe" or "out," always for a quarter. There was an okay crowd—the papers said 11,500—to check out the Browns, who were in first place for the first time since the War of 1812. To me they looked like the same old Brownies, kicking the ball around and chalking up three errors. Atley Donald went all the way for the Yanks, scattering eight hits. The St. Louis centerfielder, a guy named Byrnes who apparently suffered from glaucoma, dropped a fly ball in the third, and we scored three. In the fourth, Mike Milosevich walked and Stirnweiss hit a line drive to left, between Byrnes and a Brownie named Gene Moore, a victim of cataracts. Moore played soccer with the ball and Snuffy had an inside-the-park homer. New York finished on top 7–2, which put them 3½ behind and nobody could care less. My personal hero, Big Ed Levy, went hitless.

The game was kind of a bore after the fifth and a lot of people left early, but we stayed and so did a skinny and obvious tail-job specialist who had arrived about a half an hour after we did, just so we wouldn't get the idea he was following us. You hire somebody to tail two private dicks, you got to have your head up your ass. It was typical enough of the way the Waldorf Towers crowd had handled things to convince me immediately of what was happening. Toots had picked up on the guy as early as the third.

"The guy in the suit isn't too interested in the game," he said, looking down at his scorecard. "He went to get a couple of dogs right after Lindell doubled last inning."

I turned around and gave him a look. A sallow, black-haired number in his twenties. When I turned around, he looked at his watch. Amateur night.

"He definitely has the look, Toots."

"How do you lose somebody in Yankee Stadium?"

"You don't. And I don't want to."

"He got a reason to follow you?" asked Toots, his bushy eyebrows twitching.

"C'mon Etten, you slob!" I yelled at old Nick, after he took a hanging curve that DiMaggio would have knocked into Jersey. "He wants to test me on something, Toots, and I feel like obliging the guy."

Toots and I stood up slowly after the final out. The shadow was going out the ramp and chances were he'd pull an Elisha Cook, Jr., and stand just inside the ramp with a newspaper over his face. He fooled me: no newspaper, but rather, a complicated cigarette-lighting maneuver. Toots and I laughed out loud. He stayed about fifty feet behind us as we climbed the stairs to take the Woodlawn IRT back into Manhattan, then jumped into the crowded car with us as the doors were closing.

"We take this to Grand Central," I told Toots.

"Then what?"

"Then we go to the *Daily News* Building, which is where our friend is going to break down and cry."

The shadow intently read his scorecard all the way into the city. Toots and I stood in the vestibule, looked out over the Bronx until the train went underground, and then we just looked into the darkness, thinking our own dull and private thoughts. When we got out at Grand Central, our pal casually went out after us—yawning, that's how bored he was—and tailed us into the daylight. I turned back and observed his consternation as we stayed on 42nd and crossed Third Avenue. He started to speed up, as if to catch us, then abruptly slowed down again. As we turned into the *News* Building, near Second, Toots said, "He's running." We pushed through the revolving doors into the lobby and headed past the giant globe and war map toward the elevators.

"Wait for this guy," I told the operator, as the shadow came hurtling through the lobby.

He entered the elevator, pale and sweating.

"City desk," I told the operator. The shadow's jaw dropped.

"Don't do it," he said hoarsely.

"Do what?"

"City room, city desk. Don't tell them."

I got very close to him, close enough so that I felt sorry for him.

"Then you just stay away from me and tell our mutual friends that the next time I'm followed anywhere at all, I'll blow the whistle so loud their eardrums will pop."

"Okay, sure," he said. His light blue suit was stained and salt-marked under the armpits. "I didn't ask for this. Sounded like a dumb idea to me, but I don't have any say."

"They said to tail me and stop me if I walked into a newspaper or wire service?"

"That's right."

"Number twelve. City room," the elevator man said.

"Take us back to the lobby please," Toots told him. He said something to himself in Italian and slammed the doors shut.

We bid adieu to the tail. Toots went back to the Lava. I went home.

I listened to the Republican Convention for a while. H.V. Kaltenborn said it was wrapped for Dewey on Wednesday. First ballot for sure. The only question was the second spot: either Governor Earl Warren of California or Governor Bricker of Ohio. Then Warren himself came on to deliver the "keynote" address. Strictly craperoo: the GOP would "get the boys back home again—victorious and with all speed." I had trouble keeping my eyes open and missed entire sentences, and just managed to switch off the radio before rolling over on the couch.

When I awoke I could hear plates being scraped in other apartments and that post-dinner, pre-darkness sound of kids roller-skating in the street. I rubbed my eyes until I could make out the numbers on the hall clock. It was seven-thirty. I had been out for nearly two hours and it took ten minutes more to get off the couch and into a bent position over the sink. Cold water didn't help. I went to the kitchen and got a can of Chase and Sanborn out of the icebox. It dropped from my hands like a lead weight.

"Son of a bitch," I said to the floor. I picked the can up, put it back and walked into the bedroom. I had never felt so tired. I sat down and turned over, fully dressed, and slept until ten o'clock the next morning.

"I LET SOMEBODY INTO THE OFFICE," Eddie told me.

The elevator jockey has a set of keys to my outer office. If anyone gets there before I do, he lets him in.

"What kind of somebody?"

"Little guy with deepset eyes and a big kind of Hebe nose. Like yours."

"Thanks. He have bushy hair?"

"He'd break the comb, Mr. LeVine. Nine, all out."

It sounded like Factor and was. He was sitting in my outer office with a briefcase held tightly between his feet on the floor. A raincoat was thrown over the other chair. He was going through the morning papers—all of them.

"Hope you haven't been waiting too long."

He smiled and stood up, putting the papers aside on the little table with the pelican lamp.

"Not too long. I have to go through the papers for the chief anyhow."

I unlocked the inner office door and threw my hat on the moose head. Factor followed me in carrying his briefcase.

"I've been leading a rugged kind of life," I told Factor, sitting behind my desk and gesturing toward the easy chair. "Last night my body called a strike and I slept for thirteen hours. *After* a two-hour nap." I lit up a Lucky and offered him the pack. He shook his head and pulled out some Chesterfields. "I haven't slept like that since I was four."

"Since I went to work for the chief, oh, it's fourteen years now, I've averaged four hours a night. Once a month my body gives up too and then I conk out for the weekend. It recharges the batteries."

I smiled, he smiled, we smiled.

Factor and I blew cigarette smoke toward the ceiling. It

caught the dusty sunlight I get for fifteen minutes a day. I didn't know what was going on, but it was kind of peaceful.

"They said it was going to rain," Factor said. "But you wouldn't know it."

I looked toward the window. "Looks nice enough."

"It's a crazy world," he said, giving me a long look, what they call *significant* in the better magazines.

"Guess so," I answered, if that's an answer. "I'll make some coffee."

"That would be fine."

I ran some water into my little kettle and put it on the hot plate, then spooned some drip-grind into the pot. When I turned back to my desk, Factor was closing his briefcase.

And there was twenty-five thousand dollars on my desk. In ten packets. Twenty-five C-notes to a packet.

All for me.

"It is twenty-five thousand dollars," Factor announced, "and every cent of it is yours if you join our cause."

I picked up a packet and went through it. All hundreds.

"You may rest assured that this money is tax-free."

"But of course," I said, lifting a few more packets and methodically flipping through the bills.

"It's all there, LeVine."

I winked at him. He smiled.

"In fact, LeVine," Factor said, warming to the job, "I think I may say confidentially that as long as this Administration holds the reins of power you won't have many problems with Internal Revenue."

I picked up some more packets.

"You're telling me I don't have to pay any more taxes?"

"I'm saying you won't be bothered by the IRS if, say, your returns are pegged a little low."

"How low?"

"Well," he smiled a tight little smile and crossed his legs, "as low as you want to make them."

"That's quite an offer. What's the expiration date?"

"The offer expires, obviously, when the Democrats fall from power."

I kept counting. Factor looked encouraged.

"You're right. It's all here."

"So you're with us?"

"No. Every minute that I spend on this case I get sicker to my stomach. You walk in here, dump a pile of bills on my desk, and expect me to roll over and start wagging my tail. This isn't Washington, sweetheart. This is the big city."

He stood up, red-faced, and started shoveling the packets back into his briefcase. "If you weren't interested, why the hell did you count all of it? You like playing games?"

"I love it. And I love your persistence. What's the next offer, perpetual life?"

Factor was steaming. "There's no next offer, LeVine. You're making a very stupid blunder." He stared at me, blinking in anger and disbelief. "The mind boggles at what you're just tossing away."

"Let it boggle, then," I said, Mr. Breeze. "You know, Factor, there's one way you can buy my help."

"Which is what?" he asked cautiously.

"Which is bring me the negatives and prints of Anne Savage's films, and nobody will ever know what happened."

He stood, holding the briefcase to his chest. "You're a goddamn fool."

"Agreed, but I'm the only person in this whole gruesome world who can save your ugly face. Sit down and think about it."

He didn't sit down. In fact, he walked behind the desk and stood over me. The little guy was trembling.

"My reputation, my *prestige*, whatever you choose to call it, means nothing. The reelection of the president is the only thing that makes a damn bit of difference, because the peace and security of the whole world are at stake. Anything that returns him to the White House is worth it, is moral, is justifiable. Savage will be humiliated and he will not contribute to the Dewey campaign." The words were coming out almost mechanically, as if Factor were a wire recorder that had just gotten plugged in. "Dewey will lose and Roosevelt will win, easily. That is the only thing that matters. You and I are nothing."

"Speak for yourself and how about sitting down. I don't like people standing over me."

He sat down, the shakes all over him.

"This whole affair is ruining my health."

"All you need is a cold shower." I got up and poured some boiling water into the Dripmaster, then sat down again.

"One thing I really don't understand, Factor. If Roosevelt's reelection is so godalmighty important, why risk it by staying with a scheme that's blown up in your face?"

"What gets started gets finished," Factor said slowly. "Everything would be proceeding smoothly if you weren't in the picture."

"I'm flattered, but you're dead wrong. Shea of Homicide got pulled off two murders and he's not the kind of bird who doesn't ask why. He's a smart guy. And if he knows, maybe so do a couple of other people. It's a bust, Factor, give me the films and don't let things get worse than they are."

"You're bluffing." I could tell Factor didn't believe his own words; his eyes were doing figure eights.

"Sure, I'm bluffing. I don't know a thing. You and Butler have all the answers. Coffee?"

He nodded yes. I got up and lifted the top of the Dripmaster to make sure that all the water had drained out. When I put the top back on, a gun exploded and the pot flew from my hands, covering my pants with scalding java.

"Damnit!" I screamed and hit the floor, as another shot creased the wall over my head. I went right under the desk.

"Give up, LeVine," growled Factor, his voice choked and strange. Give up? He was playing at some cops-and-robbers fantasy, some movie he remembered. And he had demonstrated his total ineptness with a gun.

The front side of my desk was closed; to get a clear shot at me, Factor would have to come around the back. I heard his shoes shuffling around the desk, clockwise, and strained to get a grip on the front end of the desk. I waited a fraction of a second, then gave a gut-breaking heave upward.

The desk flew over and caught Factor as he was bending over, pinning him underneath and knocking the gun loose on impact. Still on my knees, I crawled across the floor to where the gun spun slowly on its side, picked it up, and started moving toward Factor. His lips formed a "no" as I got closer, smiled, and, just to seal our friendship, bashed him on the head with the butt end. It was a nice shot: hard enough to keep him dreaming about the election for a couple of hours, but placed so as to avoid doing further damage to his already crumbling mind.

I got to my feet and pulled the desk back upright, then went to the closet and donned a fresh pair of slacks, tossing the coffee-stained pair on the floor. I lit a Lucky and went wandering down the hall. A songwriter named Abe Rosen was leaning out of his office.

"Were those shots, Jack?"

"Your imagination, Abe. Probably writing a song about the war, and heard shots."

Abe was a big guy, with black hair and horn-rimmed glasses. All his shirts had "AR" emblazoned on the pockets, with a little musical note. I'd known him for a long while and he knew how to keep his mouth shut.

"But you're all right?" he asked softly.

"I'm fine."

"And the other fellow, he's dead?"

"Abe, that's Hollywood stuff. Nobody's dead, nobody got thrown out of the window. You've got brain fever."

"But if the police? . . ."

I put my arm around his shoulder. "No police, Abe. No

trouble. Go write me a little song about what a swell town New York is."

"I wrote one like that last week. You want to hear?" His eyes lit up. People usually weren't all that anxious to hear Abe's new songs. They kind of ran together in the mind. Too much moon and spoon.

"Tomorrow, Abe."

It took a lot of leaning on the bell to get Eddie off his butt.

"What's the hurry, Mr. LeVine? There's a john on the floor, ain't there?" He picked up trouble signs on my face and wised up. "You need me?"

"I need you. Can you get Vito to run this box for about a half-hour?"

"Sure. It's practically my lunch."

"Okay. Be back in my office soon as you can."

It took him about three minutes, during which I went through Factor's clothes and wallet, finding nothing of interest. Eddie walked in while I was crouched over the body.

"Christ, who's that guy?"

"Friend of mine. I want him out of here."

Eddie knelt beside me.

"He's still alive, Mr. LeVine. He's breathing."

"That's okay by me. All I did was give him a tap."

Eddie stood up and noticed the hole in the wall. His eyes widened.

"Bullet holes. He fired at you, Mr. LeVine?"

"Not very accurately. He couldn't hit Kate Smith at three feet."

"And you want me to walk him?"

"Correct. We're going to steer him out of here like he's stinko drunk, talking to him, et cetera. He'll be dragging his heels and when Lou gives us a funny look downstairs, we throw him a sheepish grin. Then I want you to take a cab over to the Waldorf Towers and leave this mug with the bellhops. Make sure they take his briefcase."

"Can we get a cab with a guy who's unconscious?"

"I'll hail the cab, then you come out with the dancing bear. It's a five-minute ride to the Waldorf. If the hack gives you any lip, tell him the guy needs medical attention."

"I don't know." Eddie seemed to hesitate. "That's a nice lump he's got there. If the cops stop us . . ."

I took a twenty out of my wallet and stuck it into Eddie's hand.

"Gee, Mr. LeVine, this is too much."

"It's to keep you from being such a sap. Stop worrying. This is a cinch."

He kept staring at the bill. "Twenty smackers. Jesus Christ. That's a week's pay, Mr. LeVine. This is a pretty big case, isn't it?"

"The biggest. Now let's get this chump into a cab."

It worked fine. Eddie and I grabbed Factor by the arms and "walked" him, legs dragging on the floor, down to the lobby. I hailed a cab tipped the driver, and told him to make sure this drunk bigwig got to the Waldorf in one piece. He knew the score, smiled and thanked me, and then actually got out of the cab to help us.

"Easy does it, boy," I told the unconscious aide to Franklin Roosevelt. "Couple cups of coffee you'll be fine."

"At least this one don't stink," said the cabbie, as he opened up the rear door.

"Two drinks and he was out," said Eddie. He looked at me and grinned, very proud of himself. I liked it myself.

The elevator jockey got in and the hack closed the door. Factor fell over on his side. I leaned in through the window.

"He's already paid," I told the kid. "And keep your eyes on that briefcase."

"I'll report back to you, Mr. LeVine."

The cab roared away from the curb.

When I returned to the office, my phone was ringing.

I recognized Madge Durham's voice.

"President Savage on the line from Chicago, Mr. LeVine."

"LeVine, how goes it?" Savage sounded crisp and confident.

"Somebody just took another shot at me, so I must be getting warm."

"Good Christ, man, are you all right?"

"They keep missing and as long as they do, I'm content."

"Should I hire a couple of bodyguards?"

"They'd just get in the way. Besides, I'm a tough guy. How's Anne?"

"She didn't make the trip," he said, matter-of-factly. Society families are wonderful. "How has my hunch about the Syndicate worked out, LeVine? You find it sound?"

"I can't give you a yes or a no yet, Mr. Savage, but I think they can be bluffed off, whoever they are."

"How?"

"I'd rather not say over the phone."

"I can understand that." He paused and there was a thin kind of whistling noise on the line. It wasn't the best connection. "Listen LeVine, I'll be in New York this afternoon. Tom will be nominated at about noon, then he'll give a speech and attend a luncheon. We expect to catch a three o'clock flight into New York. He'd like to meet you."

"Who?" I knew who and what a royal bitch it was.

"The next president," Savage chortled. "We'll be at the Sherry. Why don't you come by at around nine-thirty. That will give us a chance to freshen up a bit. We'll be in room 1807. Go to the desk and they'll have your name."

"Mr. Savage, why does Dewey want to meet with me now?"

"As you said, let's talk about it in person. I've got to run now, LeVine. I want to be at the Amphitheater when the balloting starts. Be seeing you at nine-thirty."

He hung up and I was left listening to the whistling of the

bum connection. All I needed was Dewey. Half a day after he gets nominated and he's got to see LeVine. First the Democrats and generals try to buy me off, now a nighttime rendezvous with the Grand Old Party. I didn't like it at all; it was a great big pain in the neck. Obviously, Dewey knew about the shakedown and wanted a word with the detective in charge. Just like the old days for him. Translated into the various possibilities it came out this way:

A) Savage told Dewey he felt the Syndicate was in back of the shakedown. Racketbuster Tom asks me what I think about Savage's hunch. If I say no, I have to give an alternative. If I say yes, Dewey and I go through an incredible song and dance, he throwing names and places at me, I hemming, hawing and blowing my nose. It didn't sound nice.

B) Dewey has a hunch himself, for example the right one—that the Democrats had their hands on Savage's scrotum and were squeezing. What do I think of this? Who's in back of it? Names and places, dates and faces. Once again, I have to soft-shoe or Dewey might want to blow the whole thing wide open and ride it to victory, even if Savage got a little burned.

C) Dewey just wants to pat me on the back, ask a few questions and wish me luck.

C didn't shape up too well and I thought B more an outside shot. A looked pretty good to me and it meant I'd have to go on the offensive, dream up a plan of action and avoid cross-examination. I told myself that Savage had hired me for one purpose: to stop the blackmail. Beyond that, I didn't have to say or do a goddamn thing.

I turned on my little Stromberg-Carlson and tuned in the Convention, trying to piece together some kind of battle plan for Savage. Dewey's name was placed in nomination after a couple of people had favorably compared him to Lincoln, Henry Ford, and Jesus H. Christ. I listened, thought, and filled my ashtray with a gnarled pile of cigarette butts.

Eddie knocked twice on the outside door.

"What's that, the Republicans?"

I nodded.

"Since when were you interested in politics, Mr. LeVine?" He smiled knowingly. This was a very smart kid.

"I've got nothing better to do."

"Uh huh. Hey, it worked fine. We helped him into the lobby and the cabbie said something to a bellboy. I slipped the bellboy a five and told him to get the guy and his briefcase up nice and safe."

"They ask any questions?"

"Didn't have a chance to. We dropped him off and blew."

"Perfect."

Eddie looked at me with question marks all over his kisser.

"Mr. LeVine?"

"You want to know about the briefcase?"

"Boy, you're smart. What was in it?"

"Nothing much. Just twenty-five big ones."

He whistled. "Holy Mary. He try and buy you?"

"You're close."

"And you told him to get fucked."

"Kind of."

"So he got crazy in the head and tried to shoot you. You knocked the gun out of his hand, sapped him, and it was like taking candy from a baby, right Mr. LeVine?" Eddie was smiling like a fat pussycat belching feathers next to an empty canary cage. He had a right to.

"Eddie, in about two weeks why don't you come by and we'll have a little talk. You shouldn't be an elevator jock."

"That's what I keep telling my old lady. She says I got plenty of time to be a big shot."

"Nobody's got that much time."

"You're right, Mr. LeVine. I think I got the nose to be a grade A dick."

"I think so too."

Eddie's smile was so wide it practically hung off the sides of his face. "You mean that?"

"I don't kid around about the big things, jockey, only the little ones. Give me two weeks, then we'll talk."

"I'll knock the door down."

"You going to tell your mother?"

"I guess so." He was jiggling up and down on the balls of his feet.

"What's she going to say?"

"Her?" He laughed. "She's gonna hit the ceiling, but that's all right. She'll have to learn. My old man was a barber for twenty-five years and every year he talked about opening his own shop. When he died he was still third chair at Tony's."

"He a good barber?"

"I loved my father, Mr. LeVine. He was a great guy. But he was the worst fuckin' barber in Brooklyn, no two ways about it."

We smiled at each other. It was nice to talk to a human being for a change.

"I got to go before Vito has a fit. Thanks again for the twenty."

And he was out the door, leaving me with my problems. I called Kitty Seymour and moved a dinner date we had made up a couple of hours, then pulled a beer out of the office tub. I locked the outer door, took the phone off the hook, and lay down on the musty brown couch that gets used maybe a dozen times per year. Somebody faints; I need to do some deep thinking. It's usually the former, but this afternoon required some high-grade cerebration.

It was just past one when I began. By two I felt a little better about things, and at three I started to smile.

At four o'clock I put the phone back on the hook and departed the office, feeling very good about myself.

I had an idea and it was pure genius.

If Thomas E. Dewey thought so, too, I had an even chance of living out the year.

My dinner with Kitty would have been delightful, had I been able to keep my mind in the same room with my body.

"Jack?" Kitty asked, looking a little puzzled.

"Hmm?"

"You've been holding that lobster tail in your hand for about five minutes."

"What am I supposed to do, eat it?"

She laughed. "Sounds like the suppository joke. The man buys suppositories and comes back to the druggist to complain. 'They don't work at all,' he says. The druggist's a funny guy and he says, 'What've you been doing, chewing them?' The other guy has a sense of humor, too. 'No,' he says, 'I've been shoving them up my ass.'"

I liked that joke a lot and laughed enough to turn some heads in the restaurant, The Blue Marlin.

"It's not *that* funny, Jack. You must be under a little pressure these days."

She was the smartest woman who ever lived.

"I just like suppository jokes. Always did."

"Still the chorus girl case?"

"Mmm-hmm."

"We're back to 'mmm-mmm.' The case is why you have to be somewhere at nine-thirty?"

"You're murder tonight."

"You coming over afterward?"

"If I can still walk."

"Jesus Christ. Jack?"

"What?"

"Be nimble."

HE WAS SMALLER than I had guessed: newspaper photos had led me to believe that Governor Thomas E. Dewey, the Republican candidate for president of nine hours, was about my height. I put him at around 5'9". This Wednesday night he must have felt a lot taller. His cheeks were flushed, literally, with success, his mustache was very black and sleek and neatly trimmed; his eyes were bubbling with triumph.

A Pinkerton had met me at the desk and ridden the elevator up to eighteen, then walked me to the door and disappeared. It was a little like the Waldorf set-up, except there was less officiousness and pomposity. The Waldorf aspired to class; the Sherry had it and didn't have to keep shoving it in your face. There was no butler in 1807: Savage opened the door himself. He smiled.

"Mr. LeVine, please come in."

Dewey was sitting in a corner of the living room, holding a half-filled brandy glass, looking radiant but composed. It was when he rose to greet me that I noticed the height differential.

"Jack LeVine, I'd like you to meet the next president of the United States."

"Congratulations, governor," I heard myself saying. "You must be a very proud man tonight."

"Not proud really. More awed." His voice was incredibly mellow and resonant. I had heard Dewey on the radio but that instrument couldn't capture the rich velvet of his tone. "I was telling Eli on the plane that I've never felt so humbled."

There wasn't too much I could say to that, so I didn't say anything. There was an awkward little silence which Savage filled, kind of.

"You had no trouble getting here, I hope?"

"Oh, no. Fine."

"They had your name at the desk then?" Dewey resonated.

"Oh, yes."

I couldn't quite convince myself that I was speaking with candidate Dewey and not with some stooge made up to look like him. When you come down to it, a nice chunk of the slam a public personality carries comes from his inaccessibility. You never see the guy. Carried all the way, the ultimate public figure is someone who you suspect may not exist at all. The Pope, for example, wouldn't be quite so majestic if you ran into him at Bickford's every Wednesday. Dewey wasn't all the way up there, not yet, but he was getting pretty close.

"Can I offer you a drink, LeVine?" asked Savage.

"Scotch and soda would be fine."

"Scotch and soda it is." He was Mr. Conviviality tonight. I didn't quite trust it. A show for Dewey.

"Let's sit down, shall we?" said the candidate, pointing toward the living room.

The room—drapes, rug, chairs, couch—was all cream and powder blue, with a nice discreet chandelier up on the ceiling. The white marble coffee table was covered with congratulatory telegrams and adorned by a simple vase that held about two dozen freshly cut long-stemmed roses.

"You find it a bit warm in here?"

"Not really, governor."

"Well, I do." Dewey chuckled, each chuckle weighing in at about forty kilocycles. He went to the window and opened it a bit wider, then stood looking out for a few seconds. This guy could be president. I didn't really think he had a Chinaman's chance, but sitting in the room with the guy, all I could think was White House. It's a funny thing, but being physically close to a man of that stature somehow puts you on his side. I think it's called seduction.

"Look at that," Dewey said.

I got up and went to the window. He put his arm around my shoulder.

"Can you see the hansom?"

Down there was Central Park and a horse was clopping along the road pulling a hansom cab, its driver perched motionless in top hat and tails. The hansom passed under the street lamps. It was a warm and breezy night, and couples were promenading around the duck pond.

"It's like something out of *The New Yorker*, isn't it, Jack?"

I just shook my head, trying to come up with a zinger. "A hell of a town, governor."

Dewey looked me straight in the eye, very happy. "That's right. It's a *hell* of a town, isn't it. God, how I love it."

Savage waltzed over and stuck a tall drink in my hand.

"Some view, eh, LeVine?"

"You know, Eli, standing here with Jack I just thought I couldn't put up anywhere but this suite. After the election, I'll only stay here."

"Will it be large enough, Tom?"

"Goodness, I should hope so. Two bedrooms. Secret Service can have the suite next door." He stopped and laughed. "Jack must think we're pretty cocky."

I just smiled. "It's nice to dream, I guess." It wasn't the smartest thing to say. Dewey's smile wavered for a second, but revved back up to two hundred watts after he decided the remark was innocent.

"It's no dream, LeVine," Savage said with an edge to his voice.

"No, no, I know exactly what he meant, Eli. He's right. We've got more important things to do than chatter about where President Dewey is going to stay."

The nominee returned to the couch and Savage took an easy chair. So did I. My palms were sweaty and the moisture level increased when Dewey gave me a long, searching look.

"Eli tells me you think we're making progress in this dreadful matter," he finally said.

"Some."

"Would you care to tell us where you think we stand

at this moment? You know I'm an old prosecuter so don't feel you have to pull any punches with me."

"Tom's seen it all," Savage said, taking a long swallow of his drink.

I nodded respectfully. "The latest news I can report is that an agent of the blackmail group visited me this afternoon and offered twenty-five thousand cash if I got off the case. When I turned him down, he was kind enough to take a shot at me. Luckily I spun out of the way a second before he fired or he'd have had me. I managed to shake the gun loose and knock him out."

There was a brief silence. I heard people walking past the suite: a few ladies, a few gentlemen. They were laughing politely.

"Well, that's quite a story, Jack," Dewey said. "Who do you think is pulling the strings in this operation? Eli seems to think the Syndicate might be involved. Sounds quite logical to me. As you know, I made it very hot for that crowd when I was in the D.A.'s office."

"It doesn't wash with me," I told him. "For one thing the mob doesn't go around sending one man with twenty-five grand and no one to back him up. Those boys usually do things in twos and threes."

Dewey smiled.

"I was testing you, Jack. It doesn't wash with me either."

Then Dewey turned to a door in the rear and said, "Come on out, Paul." The door opened and I wanted to get the hell out any way I could.

"A friend of yours?" Savage said, as Detective Paul Shea, Homicide, sauntered out of a rear bedroom.

"You gentlemen know each other?" asked the governor.

"We met under unfavorable circumstances." I stood up and shook hands with Shea, who kind of grunted. He was a red-haired fireplug of a man whose neck was measured in feet rather than inches. He had the blue eyes and stub nose of an Irishman, and the nicks and facial scars of a cop who always went for the fight. A couple of the teeth in his mouth were his. Paul Shea had risen in the police force on the sheer strength of his brains and muscle; he had as much Irish charm as a bagel.

"Please sit down," Savage said cheerily. "You look surprised, Jack."

"I guess I feel you don't have too much faith in me."

"Oh *really*, LeVine." Savage was taken aback by my anger. People weren't supposed to get angry at him. "It wasn't our intention to make you feel this way. Tom knows Detective Shea from his years in the D.A.'s office and called him up for a little assistance. Detective Shea raised a few questions and we thought it best to get you two together."

"The last time Shea and I got together I had double vision for a week." Shea smiled. That was his sense of humor. "And why were you hiding him in the back?"

"We weren't hiding him at all, LeVine, but we did want the chance to talk with you alone for a while."

"Confidential-like."

"Calm down, LeVine," Shea said, taking a chair. "I don't know a thing. All I got are questions. A few things happened recently that didn't take with me at all and I thought we could hash it over." His voice was a flat monotone, which made him very effective in the back room. After a while the voice itself drove you nuts.

"I know the way you hash things out, Shea. Where's the hose?"

"Be smart, shamus, you're getting upset over nothing."

"I assure you we're acting in good faith, LeVine," Savage concurred in a soothing tone.

"Story goes like this," Shea began. "A guy named Fenton got croaked after unsuccessful brain surgery in a john at the Hotel Lava. This is maybe a week ago. You know the Lava, LeVine?"

"I was bar mitzvahed there."

"I remember the affair well." He went on. "I sniff

around the Fenton murder and it checks out routine; a shake-down artist usually gets somebody mad. I wasn't very in-terested in spending my time on the case, to tell you the truth."

"I love it when you tell me the truth."

"Please, gentlemen," crooned Savage. Dewey was enjoy-ing it. Like old times.

"Stop throwing me the nasty, LeVine," said Shea. "It ain't funny." He cleared his throat. "A couple of days after this they find a corpse named Rubine stuck in a drainage pipe up in Olive, New York."

"I know Olive," Dewey contributed.

"Yessir. Well, it's this Rubine and it turns out he was in cahoots with Fenton. I went after the parley. Which is when I got yanked from the case. Suddenly nobody wants to know from nothing."

"They pulled *you* off the case, Paul?" asked the nominee.

"I was told the Olive rub-out was a matter for the local law. When I called the sheriff up there, he told me they weren't pursuing the case either."

"And *those* were the men who contacted Anne and me," declared Savage, like he had solved the whole case. "LeVine, it sounds to me like political influence is being used to throw a monkey wrench into the police investigation of this matter."

"An incredible scandal," said Dewey.

I didn't like where this was leading. Not at all.

"Let me ask you something, Mr. Savage," I finally rasped, after examining my shoes for about twenty seconds. "Do you *want* a police investigation of this case? I was under the im-pression that you wanted this matter handled without pub-licity. That's why I was hired."

"That's not the point, LeVine," said Savage. "The point is *why* were the police pulled off those homicides?" He was dead right, of course, but I was damned if I was going to tell him so.

"That's the nub of it," the candidate agreed.

"We could sew things up pretty fast if we had half a chance." Shea grabbed some brownie points.

"Sure you could and the story would be on the front page of the *News* every day for two weeks. If you folks want that, it's yours." I had to keep harping on the publicity bit or everything would get queered.

"We don't want that, of course," said the banker.

"But Jack," Dewey said in the soft tones of a priest making a house call, "who pulled the police off the case?"

"If I knew, I'd have the blackmail material. And that, gentlemen, is my only job in this case: to get that material back to Mr. Savage. That's all of it. I'm not a cop or a judge, I'm a plain old shamus who can only do one thing at a time. I've got to recover something. Whether or not anybody gets caught, or is thrown in the cooler or off a cliff, is someone else's business, not mine. Now I think I've got a way to keep everybody happy, get the materials back, and keep Mr. Savage in your campaign, governor. But I can't do a thing if I have to play guessing games with Homicide. Sorry, Shea."

Shea grunted.

"Sounds to me like you're not too anxious to have the blackmailers named, LeVine. I smell a cover-up." The son of a bitch.

"Smell what you want. My job is to do something nice and quiet. This might be a juicy case for Homicide, you boys could all get your pictures in the paper. Poring over the evidence, wagging a finger at the suspect, showing your teeth for the photogs. I don't give a damn about that. I want to get something back for Mr. Savage and I don't want the *News* and the *Mirror* drooling all over the case. I'm hired by Savage to protect Savage's interests. Period."

Shea wasn't impressed, but Savage was and that was all that counted.

"That's the sticking point, Tom."

"Governor," I said, "Shea's right. I don't care if the blackmailers are 'caught' in a conventional sense. I'm a professional who wants to have that material returned with no waves, no harm done."

"Gentlemen. LeVine's a smart boy and a good shamus, but I've got to think he knows more than he's telling." Shea spelled it out in large type.

Dewey threw me a long look.

"You have something to say to that, Jack?"

"Governor, I'm not a religious man, but let God strike me dead if I'm covering up for anyone or not acting in your best interests." I was almost ashamed of myself.

There was an embarrassed silence. Shea was unbelieving. Savage broke the stillness.

"Well, I have faith in you, LeVine. And I do want to stay out of the press."

Shea stood up.

"I guess I'm not really needed here, then. Good luck, governor. All the best."

Dewey got off the couch, put his arm around Shea's shoulders and whispered into his ear. Shea smiled and shook his head, then went to the door. As he started to open it up, he called me over.

"Jack, let's step outside for a second."

"No fighting, gentlemen," chortled the candidate, who stood a few feet from Shea, with his hands behind his back.

"Nothing like that, governor," the detective said amiably.

We stepped into the corridor.

"Nice work, LeVine. I liked that part about God striking you dead."

"I noticed tears in your eyes."

"Oh yeah? I noticed something else. A report came in this afternoon that Lee Factor was carried into the Waldorf by a hackie and an elevator boy from your building, 1651 Broadway."

"I'm fascinated."

"Funny thing, I am too. When I got pulled off those two homicides, I figured it had to be orders from on high, but how high I couldn't guess. That story about Factor starts to make sense."

"Why didn't you tell Dewey about it?"

He flashed an ice-cold grin. "Because, you miserable Jew shamus son of a bitch, I enjoy seeing you caught in the middle and mainly because I can't do a thing on this case without winding up walking the beat on Staten Island. When I'm told to lay off, I lay off. It was a risk just coming over here tonight."

"Why did you?"

"I just can't tell the governor to go fuck himself, Jack. Don't play dumb. I did my bit and now I'm going home. Also, I did you a nice favor in there."

"Telling them I was covering up? I wasn't sure that was a favor, but if it was, I'm forever in your debt."

"I knew they wouldn't go for that. But it was nice of me not to say anything about Factor."

"You just got through telling me you couldn't."

"I could have worked it in there somehow, but I didn't."

"So?"

"So maybe one of these days you'll help me clear up a couple of murders."

"Forget it, Shea. The higher-ups will never let this one see the light of day."

"FDR in on this?" he whispered, those blue eyes folding into slits.

"I don't know how high it actually goes, Paul, and that's for real. FDR may not know a thing about it. If he did, a lot of heads would have rolled already. But suffice it to say, you should forget you ever saw anybody dead in the Hotel Lava."

"I have the funny feeling you're not lying to me, LeVine. It's a unique experience."

"Enjoy it."

"I will." He stuck out his hand and I shook it. It was very hard. "You're walking on eggs, huh, LeVine?"

"On eggs on a tightrope."

"Well, don't get hurt. It's always fun to get you in the back room."

He turned on his heels and walked down the corridor. I watched him go and then reentered 1807.

Dewey and Savage were seated on the couch, speaking confidentially. I closed the door and they looked up.

"LeVine, I apologize if you thought we were attempting to interfere," Savage said as I walked back into the living room. He sounded pretty sincere about it.

"It was entirely my fault," Dewey broke in. "I called Paul and asked him if he knew of any large and powerful blackmail rings operating in the area and gave him the name of the two men who had contacted Eli. When he told me that he had been pulled off their cases, I thought it was significant and he should come up here and discuss the matter with us."

"You're right, governor. Shea's being pulled off those cases *was* significant, but not significant enough to have Mr. Savage's name become a household word in the tabloids."

"Absolutely," said the Republican nominee, and then he said it again. "Absolutely."

There was silence and the two men stared at me. Savage cleared his throat and crossed his legs.

"You said you had a plan."

LeVine's plan was fairly simple but required explanation. It also required another scotch and soda.

"My contacts with the blackmail group, gentlemen," I began, like Eisenhower standing before a map of Normandy, "have led me to believe that they are a frightened group of men who have gotten in over their heads."

"You know who they are, then?" asked Savage.

"I have a *sense* of who they are, and what their limits are, but that is different from knowing all the names and addresses. We don't need the names and addresses, as far as I can see; all we need are the films. Having discovered what I believe to be their weak points, I believe the time has come for us to go on the offensive."

"Agreed," said Dewey. He took a small cigar from his breast pocket and lit up. If he got elected, they would have to keep the windows open at the White House.

"My strategy hinges upon the blackmailers' deepest fear: that their scheme be exposed."

"It's not the Syndicate then, that's for certain," Dewey remarked. Then he hit the bull's-eye. I could tell when his eyes took fire like a bed of coals. "The Democrats."

"Good God," murmured Savage.

"Close," I said, forging ahead. "Very close. These, I believe, are friends of Democrats, but that should be obvious. If these are individuals who don't want Dewey elected, it stands to reason that they do want Roosevelt elected. That is elementary logic."

But the governor was in his own world. "We can use it My God, what an issue!"

"There's nothing to use, governor, not without getting

Anne Savage into some big black headlines. And respectfully, I really don't see an issue play here. What can you say, that Roosevelt has blackmailers on his side? What does that prove?"

"It proves a lack of moral leadership." Dewey was warming to the task. "It proves that the Democratic party is riddled with gangsterism."

"It proves nothing of the kind, governor; you're taking this way too far. Look, a lot of people are going to vote for you in November and among them are going to be wifebeaters, draft dodgers, and guys who eat with their fingers. Like I said, it doesn't prove a thing."

There was silence. Jack be nimble.

"He's right, Tom," Savage finally said. "We can't make an issue out of it without hurting ourselves."

Choruses of angels sang in my head.

"I'll admit that one or two important names are involved in this," I continued, more confidently. "The bank roll obviously has to come from somewhere and that is where we have them. Exposure for them would be as ruinous as it would for Anne Savage, more so, and like you said, governor, morality is on our side. We're not shaking anyone down. And so I propose the following, in order to keep Savage in the campaign and keep his daughter out of the papers: we will take fifteen minutes of radio time, let's say on July 4th, for an undisclosed purpose. Just take the time for an unspecified 'political broadcast.' No release to the papers, of course, just an innocuous listing in the daily radio log. Nobody will ask any questions: it's an election year, it's July 4th. Everybody figures it's just some guy who'll get on and say that Governor Dewey is a swell guy."

Dewey smiled. "I think I'm pretty good." He and Savage chuckled, two very tough Republican tigers.

"We're all great guys," I agreed, "granted. To continue: I will run off, on Dewey for President letterhead, a few copies of a press release that will explain that the distinguished

153

banker, Eli W. Savage, will speak on the topic 'Politics and Ethics: What Every American Should Know.'"

Savage paled. "We can't . . ."

"Don't worry," I told him. "You'll never give the speech."

"But we said nothing to the press," Dewey interjected. "This will get picked up. If the wire services get it . . ."

"The wires won't get it because it won't be sent to them. Perhaps a half-dozen copies will be run off and sent only to the blackmailers, who will think it's a general release and, hopefully, panic. I'll attach a note to the release which will say that receipt of the negatives and prints of the films will cancel the broadcast. That release, repeat, will only go to the black-mailers."

"Just to them," said Savage, his color returning.

"Correct. But it has to look like a general release."

Dewey puffed on his cigar.

"You sure this is going to work?"

"I'm not sure of anything. But we have to play this to the hilt. If July 4th rolls around and they think we're bluffing, they'll look up the radio listings and see that the Republicans have fifteen minutes of air time, national time. Then I suspect they'll have to do some quick thinking."

"Will there be any broadcast at all?" the governor asked.

"You feel like making a speech?"

"No, no." He waved his cigar. "It's way too early for anything like that. We can't get really going—officially, that is—until around Labor Day. It's traditional."

"Then I guess we get fifteen minutes of organ music."

Savage exhaled long and deep. Dewey got up and went to the window. I helped myself to another scotch and soda, making this one a double.

"I'm not sure I like it," the candidate said softly. "The basic idea is very, very good but . . ." he shook his head, "buying fifteen minutes of time and then canceling. That's terribly awkward, I think. Eli?"

"Very awkward," the banker echoed.

I took care of half of my drink.

"Make it ten minutes, then. Can't Savage give a straight little campaign speech, something modest?"

"No," said Savage like he meant it. "It's pointless, kicking off a campaign July 4th in wartime."

"You see, Jack," Dewey said soothingly, explaining the bad world to his little nephew, "we have until November. This is so awfully early. Plus, to start off with something vague and thrown-together, people will wonder. Look, can't we let the network know somehow that we'll probably cancel?"

"If you've got a good friend at a network who knows how to keep his mouth shut."

Savage and Dewey searched each other's faces for the answer. Savage found his first.

"Herb Feigenbaum at EAF."

Dewey hesitated. "He's for us but he still might ask questions."

"Not if you promise him plenty of paid time in the fall," I heard myself saying.

Dewey started laughing. "Have you ever thought of going into politics, Jack? God, that's perfect. He discounts this time against the certainty we won't go on the air, so he doesn't *lose* any paid time, but we get listed in the newspaper log. There's no announcement, no cancellation, and nobody knows the difference. Marvelous." Dewey was very happy.

Savage got up and made a couple of drinks. He gave one to the governor. I was killing mine more slowly. Savage lifted his glass.

"To the light at the end of the tunnel."

"And to the best damned detective in the country," Dewey added. We drank to both propositions.

I hoped they weren't unduly exuberant.

THE NEXT DAY I set about typing up my press release on ditto paper; I needed a ditto job so the release I sent out would look like one of thousands. I roughed out a few short paragraphs to my satisfaction, then waited for confirmation of the air time from Savage. He called at eleven and said that things had gone pretty smoothly with Feigenbaum, who usually drove a hard bargain. The Republicans would pay one-fifth rates for five minutes and would be listed on the log. One-fifth was very nice: Dewey must have promised the moon, come October. We were scheduled for July 4th at 10:00 P.M., WEAF in New York

A secretary in the building across the way noticed a run in her stocking and pulled her skirt way up to inspect it. I inspected with her, then turned back to the release. I wanted it finished before noon.

The end result sounded good enough to take ten years off Factor's life.

SAVAGE TO SPEAK JULY 4TH:
POLITICS AND ETHICS THE SUBJECT

Eli W. Savage, president of the Quaker National Bank of Philadelphia, will deliver a radio address, "Politics and Ethics: What Every American Should Know," on Tuesday, July 4th, at 10 P.M. over the Blue Network, WEAF in New York.

Mr. Savage supports the candidacy of Governor Thomas E. Dewey, whose "courage, youth and honesty are vital for the shaping of the postwar world." His radio address will touch on the need for ethical and moral leadership in the nation, "qualities in which the Democratic party has proven woefully deficient."

I phoned it in to Savage, who cleared it with the candidate and gave me the green light ten minutes later.

"Tom said something, though, LeVine, and I think he may be right."

"What?"

"He's afraid the blackmailers will think it's a bluff when they don't see the story picked up in the press."

"Who'd pick this up? It's a routine puff, a piece of campaign flackery."

"I'm not so sure, LeVine. It's an ominous little release."

"It's ominous only because you know what's behind it. And besides, the nuances aren't important because the newspapers aren't going to get the story anyhow. It's academic. The important thing is that when the blackmailers call EAF and ask if there's a political broadcast on July 4th at ten, a little man will leaf through his books and tell them yes. That is when it will get interesting."

"I suppose so."

"Of course. Tell the governor what I told you. He keeps forgetting that the release isn't actually going out. God knows these mugs aren't going to call the papers themselves and start asking questions. And look, I need that letterhead."

"A messenger is bringing it over."

"Fine. You staying in New York, Mr. Savage?"

"Oh no, LeVine, it's a little more than I can bear right now. I'll return to Philadelphia this afternoon and come back Monday night, if necessary. I do hope the films are in our possession before then."

"I hope so, too, but don't count on it. Chances are you'll have to come back."

"What a son of a bitch this turned out to be, didn't it, Jack?" He sounded very tired all of a sudden.

"It'll be over soon."

"Yes," he said vaguely and then hung up. I was left holding the phone and taking another look at the secretary across the way. She noticed and threw me a finger.

A messenger boy brought me the Dewey letterhead about a half-hour later. I signed a slip while he picked at a walnut-sized pimple on his neck. Very pretty, it almost brought my breakfast up. There are certain things LeVine finds stomach-wrenching and this kid was hitting the bull's-eye.

When he left, I went on down the hall and knocked on Abe Rosen's door. He opened up with a sleepy smile.

"It's Bulldog Drummond."

"Hope I didn't spoil your concentration, Abe." I walked in. "Where's the blanket and pillow?"

"So I took a little nap. Crucify me. You want the machine?" he asked, seeing the sheet dangling from my hand.

"Yeah. It working?"

"It always works. What are you running off?"

"No show, Abe. Not this time."

"No keyhole report this time? I observed Mrs. Rappaport performing an unnatural act upon a horse in room 604 at the Hotel Cumstain."

"You left out what kind of horse."

"Palomino. Let me look, Jack. I love those things." He looked over my shoulder.

I turned and held the sheet behind my back.

"Abe, gimme a break. I can't. Do Jack a favor and look out the window while I run this thing off. It'll take a minute."

He realized I wasn't kidding.

"This got something to do with those shots yesterday?"

"You mean the firecrackers?"

"Check, the firecrackers. Same case, Jack?"

"Same one, Abe. Now be a sweetheart and turn around for a minute. Look at the girls out the window."

"That's all I've done this morning. That and sleep." He turned around slowly, like a revolving ashtray. Which is sort of what he was. People in the music business called him a "decent guy." In that racket "decent guy" is the kiss of death.

I ran off five copies and quickly checked them.

"Okay Abe, you can come out."

He looked over his shoulder.

"You're sure I don't have to stand here all day?"

"Only if you want to."

He walked me to the door. "I'll go back to sleep. Thanks for breaking up my day a little."

Back in the office, I typed a personal note to Factor.

Dear Lee,

Savage will blow the whistle over a nationwide hook-up on July 4th, unless the prints and negatives are returned before that date. He feels his reputation can only be enhanced by such a show of integrity. And, of course, it ensures a Dewey victory.

It's all over, Lee. Return the material to my office.

Hoping your head feels better,

I am . . .

It was a good note. I liked it, particularly the "of course" at the end of the first paragraph. It wasn't every day that I could "ensure" a presidential election. After patting myself on the back, I attached the note to a press release and folded both inside an envelope marked "Lee Factor, Waldorf Towers, URGENT." Then I grabbed my hat off the moose head and locked up.

The day had turned clammy and the sky was getting so dark that the cars were going to their parking lights. I got a cab to the Waldorf and managed to drop off the envelope, buy a *Sun,* and duck into a coffee shop before the rains came. They broke a minute after I got inside, the raindrops clattering noisily against the window panes.

"Uh, oh," said the red-haired waitress, taking a gander out the window. Her features were carefully held together by powder, rouge, and hope. Slap her on the back and her face would fly off.

"Everybody's gonna order in," she said.

"Tough break."

"It's life."

I dropped the subject, whatever it was, ordered a meat loaf platter, and unfolded the *Sun.* Good news was in abundance: the Russians looked ready to recapture Minsk, LeVine's ancestral homeland, and the Allies were sweeping toward Siena and Le Havre. The rest of the front page was all Dewey: one of the youngest nominees in history, a meteoric rise, a genuine challenge to Roosevelt's fourth-term hopes. Some controversy over the nomination of Bricker for veep, but conservative elements in the Party are pleased, and it gives geographical balance to the ticket.

The Yankees lost. The Dodgers lost. The Giants lost.

After the meat loaf arrived, I ate very slowly, delicately halving even the french fries. The rain was torrential. People ran hunched through the streets, pressing newspapers to their heads. Fresh ink ran off the sides in black rivulets. Umbrellas got turned inside out and a trash can across the street was bristling with their upturned handles. Clusters of people waited in doorways. They looked at their watches and at the sky. The coffee shop was only half-filled at 12:45.

By my third cup of coffee and the funny pages, the rain was letting up and the sun was shining through its last drops. I paid my tab and left to go out on the slick, wet streets. A waterfall ran off the coffee shop's awning. People were venturing out of the doorways, smiling. It had been a hell of a rain.

My phone, of course, was ringing by the time I reached the office. I knew the ringing wouldn't let up, so I took my sweet time unlocking the inner office door and casually tossed my hat on the moose head.

Lee Factor was practically incoherent.

"LeVine? LeVine?"

"LeVine here."

"Is this possible, this nonsense I just got in an envelope. How dumb can you be? How dumb can any human . . . to think that a half-assed stunt like. . . . Listen, who do you think you're dealing with here—answer me—some guy from the sticks, somebody you caught fucking a chicken? Listen to me. Savage on the radio telling America his daughter made blue movies in Holl. . . . Listen to me. It's a joke. I almost feel sorry and that's the truth. I almost feel sor . . ."

"Why don't you take a cold shower, Lee? I can't make out a word you're saying."

I hung up and picked my teeth until the phone rang again.

"What's the meaning of hanging up on me? What's. . . . I represent the president of the United States of America."

"Remind me to change my citizenship."

"What's the meaning of that? What's this press release? What is it?"

"Read it."

"I've read it a lot. Savage is making a ridiculous speech over nationwide radio."

"Correct. Return the prints and negatives and he won't. Don't and he will. It's as clear and simple as the blue, blue sky."

"Don't talk cutesy with me, LeVine. It doesn't become you, not a bit. And neither does this release. I thought you had brains. I thought you had guts. But this dumbass . . ."

I had had enough.

"Quit wasting my time! If you think the release is a fake call up EAF and ask them what's on their log for July 4th at ten. Why should we bluff if we've got you by the nuts?"

"That's very funny, LeVine. Very, very funny, in fact. Savage's entire reputation is at stake, his vast apparatus shaken by a slimy scandal like this, and you've got *us* by the nuts? You're a comedian."

"Fine. I'm a comedian. He'll go on the radio, admit to an indiscretion on the part of his young daughter, since reformed, and indict the Democratic party to such an extent that FDR couldn't carry the Bronx against Hitler. Your neck's in a noose, Factor, so don't bore me with threats to Savage's reputation. It's the bunk. Return those films and save yourself a lot of heartache. Be thankful you have an out."

His voice went weird.

"Thankful," he whispered. "You'll never have the satisfaction. The films stay with me. There's no radio show. You understand?"

He hung up. Straitjacket City and I didn't like it at all. Factor was crazy enough to hold on to the films at all costs. "You'll never have the satisfaction." Like a bank robber trapped on a rooftop, or a captain standing with his arms folded as his ship checks out for keeps. Factor was capable of ripping up the release and telling no one about it. I called the Waldorf and asked if General Redlin was still there. They put me through to his suite. A lady answered. Some lady.

"Yes?" she sang. The voice was the richest honey of the brightest Southern flower.

"Hi, honey. Is General Redlin there?" She giggled girlishly and put her hand over the mouthpiece. When she spoke, she was still giggling. "He's indisposed."

"I can imagine. Tell him to get his pants on and come to the phone. It's Jack LeVine."

She wasn't offended in the least, not this tootsie.

"I should say you've got quite a nerve but you sound like a perfect darling," she crooned. Then she called over to Redlin. "General, it's someone named Jack Levine."

"LeVine," I told her. "Like Hollywood and Vine."

"You from Hollywood, honey?"

Redlin grabbed the phone.

"Hello, LeVine?" he barked.

"Who's she, the third front?"

"You call to be smutty?"

"I called to do you a favor. I think Factor's brains are turning to applesauce."

"He's high-strung."

"Is that what they call it in the army? Yesterday he took a shot at me."

"WHAT?" Redlin's teeth practically came through the mouthpiece.

"He missed by a mile but it's the thought that counts. Today I sent him a press release concerning Eli Savage's radio speech and he went flat crazy over the phone."

"Radio speech? LeVine, I don't know what the hell you're talking about."

"Savage is going to tell the whole story over a national hook-up unless the films are returned by July 4th. Factor didn't tell you?"

"No he didn't."

"That figures. You have a courier at your disposal, I trust?"

"Naturally."

"Send him to my office. 1651 Broadway. I'll give him a copy of the release."

The courier, a ramrod-straight lad of about twenty, arrived within ten minutes. He knocked twice, walked in and stood at attention before my desk. He saluted.

"At ease," I told him. "It's on the desk."

He clicked his heels and picked the envelope off the desk, then saluted again, turned on his heels and exited. I laughed out loud and began my wait for a response.

It turned out to be a very long wait.

THURSDAY PASSED BY soundlessly. I tried Redlin late in the afternoon and was told he was in conference. I called Quaker National in Philly and informed Miss Durham that she could tell her boss the situation was unchanged. I asked her how Anne was. She told me that Anne was on a slow train to the Savage mountain retreat in Aspen, Colorado, where she would remain for the rest of the summer.

"Sounds like a good idea."

"Mr. Savage would like you to be his guest there at the conclusion of this case."

"The successful conclusion."

"We trust it will be successful."

"Can I bring a friend?"

"Of course." Then she surprised me. "If you had no friend, the president would have provided one."

"At what interest?"

You'll love her comeback. "I'll give the president your message."

That was Thursday.

Friday morning was spent going through my files, chuckling over old reports, looking at my watch and staring at the phone. It sat on my desk as silently as a brick. Around noon I broke down and tried Redlin, only to be again told that he was tied up in meetings.

Friday afternoon. My office was so dead the moose head must have thought it was midnight. Savage called once, less than delighted over developments. I told him to sit tight.

The weekend was the long Independence Day break, a four-day affair. Kitty and I went to Rockaway on Saturday, along with everybody else, and managed to find a postage stamp of beach on which to place our folding chairs. We held hands and went into the water. It was pretty cold; Kitty squealed prettily and I hopped up and down, and was glad to get out again. Teenagers played "running bases" in the sand, we laughed at the fat men in their droopy trunks, and a handful of bathing beauties showed off their bodies, making their boyfriends very proud. There were lots of children shrieking and weeping, a lot of parents cupping their hands around their mouths and shouting names. We ate hot dogs and our soft drinks spilled noiselessly into the sand. Gulls flapped about and the waves made that noise that makes you feel so small. America. Rockaway. Fourth of July. You know all about it, that mixture of ease and pain. You try to relax completely but your failures infiltrate the heat and the blue sky. Past mistakes and dead relatives share your blanket.

In the evening, Kitty and I went to see an okay movie with Red Skelton and Esther Williams. We sat in the balcony and necked, then went home and made a lot of love.

"You need a woman's touch in this house, LeVine," Kitty told me. I covered her mouth with a kiss, and we laughed and rolled over again.

I managed to keep the case out of mind while listening to the Yankee–White Sox doubleheader on Sunday. Kitty read the paper, did the crossword, listened to the phonograph. We found ourselves retiring to the bedroom once more.

"This is starting to get interesting, shamus," she whispered into my ear.

"You are good company," I told her. "You'd probably always be good company."

Then the phone rang and the holiday was over.

"LeVine?" It was Factor. His voice was unmistakable, despite a loud humming over the line.

"Where are you calling from, Factor? This is a terrible connection."

"It's not important." He sounded tenser than ever. "Listen,

I understand you attempted to contact General Redlin on two occasions Friday."

I said nothing.

"Is that true?"

"A bookie friend asked me to call him and get odds on the battle for Minsk."

"Redlin's out of the picture, LeVine."

"What means 'out'?"

"'Out' means the South Pacific. He and General Watts were ordered back there yesterday."

"Is that why you called, to clear the order with me?"

"I'm laughing, LeVine. I am on the floor. I called to relay that information because I suspected you figured Redlin to be the weak link in the operation, the man whose fears you could play upon. And you figured right, LeVine. Your instincts were correct. He is a military man, not a politician. He does things precisely, he plays the percentages, he stays away from high risks."

"Not like you."

"Goddamn right not like me. I'm in this for keeps."

"At the risk of repeating myself, I can't see how a couple of stag movies are worth giving the election away. It doesn't make sense."

"It makes sense because there won't be any speech."

"Factor, I cannot believe you are serious. This is absolute insanity on your part."

He gave me a nasty little laugh.

"You'll see how serious I am, LeVine. By the way, your friend Warren Butler took a slow boat to Paraguay last night. He's going to be an ambassador. You see what executive power means? What you can do?"

"It's marvelous. I hope the young men of Paraguay have been forewarned. Sodomy should make great advances down there."

"You know what you are, LeVine? A goddamn moralist.

All you private dicks are the same: tough talk and bullshit on the outside. Inside, you're a bunch of old ladies."

"You're a crazy man," I said.

"Good night" was what he said.

23

TUESDAY NIGHT at eight o'clock, Savage sat in my office, ashen with worry. It was the Fourth of July.

"I knew this would happen. They've got us with our pants down."

He was sitting in the overstuffed client's chair that faces my desk. When he lit up a pipe, I could see how very shaky he was. I thought of Kerry Lane's first visit, ages ago. We had come full circle.

"And you're definitely unwilling to spill the beans tonight?"

The remaining color drained from his face. Even his hair seemed to turn whiter.

"But we don't really have the air time."

"We could still take it."

He thought that one over. "Do we have the evidence to make it stick? Hard evidence?"

That was the show-stopper: there were no letters, nothing signed, nothing deposited.

"Warren Butler was part of this, Mr. Savage, and he was named ambassador to Paraguay today. That looks suspicious."

"Suspicious isn't enough." He paused. "Butler the producer?"

"The producer of Anne's show."

"Incredible." Savage shook his leonine head. "LeVine, my name is money. Literally. Even to brush it with scandal would have the gravest economic and monetary repercussions. I just can't have it."

He was starting to fly off the handle and I had to get him back on, if we were going to survive the night.

"Okay, forget it. I understand your position completely. You're right."

"It's not just me, LeVine. If we can't prove this thing beyond a shadow of a doubt, then Tom looks like a damn fool. He has to be a statesman."

"Not a rackets prosecutor."

He permitted himself a small smile. "Exactly. I assure you we talked this all out yesterday. Tom realizes that making blackmail charges would cast him in a role he played six or seven years ago. But now he's running for president, and in wartime. He's going to be dealing with Churchill and Stalin, for God's sakes. He can't go around making wild charges."

"He can't make a gangbusters play is what you're saying."

"Precisely so." Then his eyes went sad and his jaw slackened. "What do we do, then?"

I lit up a Lucky and inhaled for as long as I could.

"We go to Radio City, take the elevator up to the twenty-sixth floor and proceed to studio 6H. We stand in back of a microphone and wait until 10:00 P.M. By which time, I believe, the films will be in our possession."

"Why haven't they been returned before now?"

"Because these guys are apparently playing chicken. They can't believe you'd actually go on the air and expose your daughter. They figure the 'political broadcast' to be just a puff for the governor. When they see you go in, that's when it'll hit the fan."

Savage puffed on his pipe and gazed into its smoke, as if searching for guidance.

"Do you think they might try to prevent us from entering the studio?" His speech was slow and thoughtful.

So was mine.

"Yes. Definitely."

He didn't blink. "I see."

"What kind of physical shape are you in, Mr. Savage? No heart condition or anything? I ask because we might have to do some running tonight."

"I work out daily and my physician says I have the body

of a forty-year-old man. You know I'm fifty-two," he concluded, proudly.

"Fine, then we average out. I'm thirty-eight and have the body of a fifty-year-old."

He permitted himself a genuine belly laugh over that. I was glad to see him loosen up a bit.

"Oh, I'm sure you're jesting, LeVine. I saw you come flying through my window that day. You seemed very fit."

I stood up. "I'll manage."

"We ready?" he asked.

"I think we'd better go. You have a car here?"

"Of course."

"Tell your driver to get lost for a while. At five past ten he's to meet us in front of Radio City, that's 50th just east of Sixth. Tell him to keep the doors open and the motor running."

"And for now we'll walk?"

"It's only a couple of blocks. And I think we should stay on our feet from here on in."

It was a warm evening, but the sweat that streamed off my body and formed little pools in the hollows above my BVD's was more than the heat warranted. We left the building at around 8:30, with the sky just beginning to darken. I had memorized the evening radio schedule on WEAF:

7:30—Dick Haymes Show
8:00—Ginny Sims
8:30—"A Date with Judy"
9:00—Mystery Theatre: "Bunches of Knuckles"
9:30—World at War: Carl Van Doren
10:00—Pepsodent Show: Charlotte Greenwood, with Marty Malneck, his band, and the famous "Hits and Misses"

If we had time, I'd like to hear "Bunches of Knuckles." It had a nice ring to it. I mentioned the show to Savage and he smiled wanly. His jaw was set and a little vein in his temple was more prominent than it had been before.

The sidewalks were thick with people and kids. The children, many of them holding little flags, were starting to yawn. The sun had vanished for keeps, day was yielding to night.

And we were two blocks from Radio City. Neither of us was speaking now. No little jokes or tension-breakers. Everything was at stake. Savage almost stepped in front of a cab and I had to pull him back.

One block and Savage's nerves were stretched tighter than bridge cables.

But he had nothing on me. Not after I stopped on the west side of Sixth Avenue, looking east.

The entrance to Radio City was surrounded.

"Jesus H. Christ," I said, nearly to myself.

"What is it, LeVine?" asked Savage.

"Take a gander at the animal life in front there."

Some very familiar thugs, heavies, and free-lance muscle were crowding the doors leading to the studio building. I recognized the Rover Boys who had waited for me on that afternoon in Sunnyside, and the tall and silent men who had infested the lobby of the Waldorf. All stood looking up and down the street, their eyes peeled, their hands stuck deeply and ominously in their pockets.

They were waiting for us.

I pulled Savage into the entrance to a Blarney Stone corned-beef-and-booze joint.

"You see someone you recognize?" he asked me.

"There's an army of thugs nesting outside the doors. Some of them I know, the others I don't want to know."

He removed a handkerchief from his handsome navy blue suit and mopped that elegant brow. "This, as they say, is the cutting edge."

"Whatever," said the detective.

"What's their game, LeVine? Kidnap?"

"Too much possible publicity. They'll try and detain us."

"Do we turn back or make a run for it?"

"Neither. If we run, we're as noticeable as camel drivers. Not to go is out of the question."

"If we hold flags," Savage said with a grim smile, "perhaps they'll mistake us for tourists."

It was fantastic.

"You're a genius, Mr. Savage."

He shook his head. "I was joking, Jack. It was an idiot idea."

"The flags were, but not the tourist bit. We'll get on a sight-seeing bus. They all stop at Radio City."

"How do we get one from here?"

"Don't move from this spot until I wave you over."

I pulled my hat low over my brow and fought past the crowds. It wasn't such a long shot: the buses stopped at Radio City every half-hour or so, so the hicks could tour the radio studios and see a show. We would blend right in. The problem was time.

And then it wasn't. When I peered down 50th Street, I immediately saw a big beautiful Gray Line Special with lots of glass and SIGHT-SEEING and fifty rubes craning their necks for a glimpse of Walter Winchell crossing the street with a "Press" card in his hat and a notebook in his hand. The bus was moving slowly down the block as the light turned green. No good. I could never flag it down.

The light wasn't a very long one, but the Gray Liner was only six cars away from it and moving. Five cars. Three cars.

Suddenly a cab, bless its miserable driver's heart, stopped dead in the center of the street to pick up a fare. The fare took his own sweet time as the bus driver leaned on his horn. The hackie got the fare, turned off his roof light and moved up. The bus followed.

Still green. Now green and red. Turning. Now red. The cab ran the light and the bus jolted to a stop. The driver's window was open.

"You stopping at Radio City," I called to him.

He turned his head and stared at me, a toothpick jutting from the side of his face. Except for the lumber, he looked well-groomed, even theatrical.

"Last stop, bud."

"Let me on." I whipped out my inspector's shield. "Police business." I started sweating the green light again.

"Sorry, can't." He turned away.

"One block, official business. Me and the lieutenant."

"I don't understand. You on the level?"

I decided to get angry.

"I'm on the level and there's nothing to understand, not when it's official police business." Light was still red. "You double-park these boats all over town and we give you more breaks than you're worth."

He grinned. "I guess you guys have done me some favors." Then he leaned over and the door squeaked open on the other side. The light turned green. I ran around the front and waved over Savage. He came over double-time. Cars started honking.

"Hurry up, eh?" said the driver.

Savage got in, I followed, and the driver slammed the door shut.

A bus full of hayseeds gazed at us. Savage and I went to the back and grabbed a couple of seats.

"Christ almighty," he whispered.

"It'll work. It'll work."

The bus rolled across Sixth and slowly came to a stop outside Radio City. The driver pulled down a little hand mike.

"Ladies and gentlemen, your last stop on the Gray Line Blue Ribbon Tour of Manhattan is fabulous Radio City in Rockefeller Center, where many of your favorite radio programs are broadcast each and every night. We'll have the pleasure of touring the actual radio studios."

Oohs and ahs from the hicks—mainly middle-aged and dressed to floor the big city. I took a peek out the window. We were parked right at the entrance.

"Take a look," I told Savage.

They were in raincoats, bulging raincoats, these men with the bent noses and cauliflower ears, the palookas, the schtarkers. Others were less obvious: clean-looking, if thick-necked, candidates for the G-Man Training Center.

"How do we get off?" whispered the banker.

"Slowly, and in the middle of the group. When we go through the doors, we accelerate and go for the first open elevator door."

"Tonight, for example," the driver went on, "we'll have the special privilege of attending a live broadcast of none other than that sixty minutes of music and fun, 'The Pepsodent Hour.'" This guy thought he was Harry Von Zell, and the explosion of noise that followed his announcement was incredible: a din and babble and chatter of such force that a couple of the uglies looked up into the bus.

"Get down," I hissed.

Savage and I hunched over in our seats. A couple across the aisle stared at us like we were Loeb and Leopold.

"Police business," I whispered to them. "Please act naturally."

The couple turned and faced forward, little smiles fixed on their faces. Husband, a fat baldie of about fifty, whispered to Wife, a garden rake of the same age, and she chuckled and shook her head. Big doings in the Big Apple.

"Seats for these broadcasts are hard to come by," said the driver, "but your Gray Line ticket includes a reserved seat—front row center—for 'The Pepsodent Hour.' So, if you will, we're running a little late, step lively out of the bus and follow me into the lobby. We'll tour the fabulous Radio City broadcast facilities and then air time, Pepsodent time, is ten o'clock."

Everybody started scrambling out of their seats, including the president of the Quaker National Bank and myself. We elbowed our way into the middle of the group, in back of an obese and varicose-veined lady of around sixty.

"How come you come in so late?" she demanded of me.

"Police business," I said, lips barely moving. "Face front and you don't know me from Adam." I bit the words off. Her eyes got a little crossed and she turned toward the front.

"Jesus Christ," Savage whispered into my ear.

"We take it nice and easy," I told him from the corner of my mouth. The group started forward. We got near the front.

"Anyone looking?" the banker murmured as we neared the doors.

"Not that I can see. They don't even see these buses, take them for granted."

Savage and I got off and kept our faces held rigidly to the front. The thick-necked men were either scanning the street or whispering into each other's ears.

We followed the other tourists like elephants plodding around a circus ring, trunk to tail. It took maybe three seconds to reach the doors and we were a half-second away when I heard a hoarse bellow: "THAT'S THEM—WITH THE RUBES!"

"Move it," I snarled at Savage, and we pushed hard through the revolving doors. I knocked the fat lady over and reached out to guide Savage around her fallen carcass. When I looked over my shoulder, four or five of the gorillas were frantically groping their way through the three sets of doors.

"They're coming, LeVine," gasped the banker.

"Time to use that forty-year-old body. Straight ahead!"

We sprinted across the black marble floor at full tilt, heading toward a bank of elevators that stood thirty yards away. The lobby at Radio City consists of a lot of small shops divided by long corridors broken by regularly spaced banks of elevators, eight to a set.

Tourists choked the corridors and we kept knocking people around, drawing shouts and curses that fell on stone ears. The murals on the wall—MIRACLE OF RADIO, OPENING OF ERIE CANAL—swam past in a pastel blur. The thugs were gaining. There were fifteen yards, tops, separating us.

"Oh God, LeVine," Savage said suddenly.

At which point a phalanx of wounded vets, in uniform, came rolling in wheelchairs from a side corridor and blocked us off. Behind them, two more rows were moving forward with surprising speed. The men looked pleased at their progress. A nurse smiled at us.

"Please let us through," I croaked.

"What?" She didn't understand. Nobody understands simple English words at moments like that. It's just too difficult.

A vet heard us though and brought his chair to a quick stop, leaving a gap of maybe two feet. I raced through, holding Savage like a pull toy, and steamed toward the first bank of elevators. As we passed through, I heard a dull metallic noise as the wheelchairs closed their ranks again.

I turned to see our pursuers blocked off, six men with mashed-potato faces rendered helpless by an armada of wheelchairs. The vets were coming out in pairs now: a double phalanx of steel and spokes. I continued running, just as the vets broke ranks again and let the thugs through. Two of them squeezed past and turned on the speed.

We reached the elevator bank. All the doors were closed. No lights were on. The next bank was another thirty yards away.

"God almighty!" I tugged at Savage and turned down the corridor. The two men were twenty feet behind us. We ran hard. Savage knocked down a child and almost stopped, but I pulled at him. We were five yards from the next set when I heard a voice saying "going up" and saw a pair of doors closing.

"Hold it," I bellowed and practically carried Savage into the elevator. The car was jam-packed.

"Comfortable?" the jockey crooned.

"Let's go," I grunted.

"He's giving orders," he joked to the others in the car. They chuckled appreciatively. "I love it when people give me orders."

The two gorillas turned the corner and raced toward the elevator. My heart had stopped beating.

"Sorry gentlemen, full up," the jockey told the uglies, then powered the doors shut before they could stick their paws into the car.

We started up, taking the first twenty floors nonstop. My ears popped. I turned to Savage and smiled.

"A lively start."

He returned the smile, but weakly. There he was, immaculately dressed in a navy blue suit with the faintest gray striping, a superbly raised, educated, and groomed man of fifty-two, on the lam. It was a novel experience for Savage, and he was handling it better than I had any right to expect.

"I feel terrible about the child," he said, wiping his brow with a spotless hanky. "He went down hard."

"He bruised his knee. Stop worrying. You haven't seen anything yet."

The elevator was full of tourists, agitated at the prospect of gaping at an actual radio broadcast. Most of them got out at twenty-five, where engineering facilities and dressing rooms were located. Savage and I stepped aside to let them out. I felt myself tensing up all over again as the jockey took the short hop up to twenty-six. Savage bit his lip.

We emerged on twenty-six looking for Studio 6H. I had called Feigenbaum that afternoon to let him know Savage and I would actually be there. He had been confused—why appear, if no broadcast? I had told him an appearance was necessary, period. He said he'd be in 6H, waiting.

In Studio 6A, "A Date with Judy" was going out over

the airwaves and a thirtyish doll with a blonde rinse was making like a fifteen-year-old bobbysoxer. Four men and a woman were standing in back of microphones over in 6B, getting ready to do "Mystery Theatre." They thumbed through their scripts, joked with each other and with the engineers. It looked like more fun than the real thing. I wanted to tell them so. 6C was a little room used for news broadcasts.

And then there was 6D, a huge, drafty room used for live audience broadcasts and the site of "The Pepsodent Show." Some musicians were already up in the bandstand, tuning up and swapping dirty stories. My destination, 6H, was actually off 6D, but in order to get there you had to go the long way, around the "L" of the corridor to its end.

Savage and I turned the corridor.

They were all over the place: more muscle, more black shirts and white ties. They stood around casually, chatting with each other or just cracking their knuckles.

"Get back," I whispered to the banker, but he had turned the corner and was spotted.

"It's him," someone shouted.

"This way." I grabbed Savage and pulled him to a fire door a few yards away.

We ran through the door and down the stairs, yanking open a bulky door and emerging on the twenty-fifth floor. A pretty guide was leading a gaggle of hayseeds through the wonders of radio. They walked down the sleek, well-lit corridor toward us.

"Right this way," the freckled redhead was saying, "are the dressing rooms, used by performers who take part in those programs done before a live audience. Tonight, for example, the stars of 'The Pepsodent Show,' Charlotte Greenwood, Marty Malneck, and the Hits and Misses will all make up in these very dressing rooms."

Behind us, I heard heavy footsteps clumping down the stairs, two at a time.

"Dressing room," I told Savage and pulled him by the sleeve. We streaked down the corridor, to the delight and laughter of the tour group, who thought it was staged for their benefit. The guide, with her turned-up nose, examined us quizzically, then led the group past the fire door, just as it opened. Two burly men emerged and looked from side to side. Savage and I, obscured from view by the herd of tourists, flattened ourselves against the wall. The two men ducked back down the stairs.

Savage and I walked into the dressing room, a long narrow area broken up by partitions. It was deserted.

"Let's sit in the back," I said.

We sat down heavily on a bench, breathing hard.

"LeVine, this is impossible," Savage finally gasped. Sweat glistened in fine diamonds on his forehead. "We're blocked off. Let's just try and get out in one piece."

"The hell with that. We've gotten this far. All we have to do is get into that big studio, cut through a small stretch of corridor and we're in. It's a matter of timing."

"But they spotted me the second . . ."

The door of the dressing room swung open. I held my breath.

A young man entered, a scrubbed and combed lad of perhaps twenty. He wore a red-and-white candy-striped sports jacket, white slacks, and white shoes. A straw hat adorned his head.

"Can I help you?" he asked pleasantly.

I stood up. "LeVine, Associated Press," I told him, flashing one of my numerous press cards. "And my partner, Smokey Savage. You with the Hits and Misses?"

He nodded. "Since last year. Sit down, please, gentlemen." He pulled over a chair. "I was 4-F and always thought I could carry a tune. Came down here from Hartford, auditioned for the H & M and they took me right on. You doing a story on us?"

"I'd like to. A Sunday piece." I fingered the sap in my pocket.

"Well, let me see what I can tell you." He got up and spun around, holding his hands against the back of his neck. He was a sweet kid, if a little fey. I didn't enjoy stepping forward, pushing his hat over his eyes and cracking him on the back of the skull.

"JACK!" gasped Savage.

The kid was on the floor, good for an hour of rest and a day of headaches.

"Had to be done, Savage. Help me with the suit. It'll fit you like a glove."

Savage knelt beside me. "You expect me to . . ."

"It's the only way we're going to get in there."

"We're both going to dress up?"

"Of course. Next kid comes in, I'll have to sap him, too. Means and ends, Mr. Savage. It's a bad world. Now let's step on it."

In two minutes, Savage was a Hit and Miss, and junior was sleeping in a broom closet with a gag in his mouth.

"He'll stay out?" asked the banker, who had gotten quickly accustomed to knocking people unconscious. He stood in front of a full-length mirror. The outfit was a little small, but not enough to draw any stares.

"God, this is ridiculous," he said to the mirror.

"It'll do. Stay out of the way, back of the partition. I don't want you spotted."

Savage ducked out of sight just as the door opened again. Another Hit and Miss waltzed in, this one a little longer in the tooth than the first victim of LeVine's duplicity.

"Who the hell are you?" he asked.

"Jack LeVine, AP."

"AP?" He didn't believe me any more than if I had said I was Sam Goldwyn. "C'mon, take a powder."

"You don't like newspapermen?"

"I don't like shit artists and I can always spot one. I

don't know what you want and I don't care. People come in here . . ."

A knee in the groin slowed him to a gentlemanly walk, the sap finished him nice and easy. Savage came out and dragged off the Hit's clothes, gagged him and locked him into the crowded closet. We were getting pretty good at it.

"I didn't know this was going to be so damned ugly," Savage said softly, as I hopped out of my slacks and into the white ducks. I put on the shirt, bow tie and jacket, then squeezed into the shoes, before putting my clothes up on a hanger.

"Fucking shoes," I mumbled.

"Too small?"

"It'll look like I'm walking on coals."

We walked—Savage walked, I hobbled—to the door. The banker turned around.

"Will our clothes be safe?"

"Probably. It's the least of our worries. You have your wallet?"

"Certainly."

"Then we're set." I inhaled and let all the air out of my body. Savage put his hand on the door knob.

"LeVine, no matter what happens, I'll be forever grateful for the imagination and courage . . ."

"Save it. I'm being well paid. Now let's blow before another one of those monkeys comes in here. And put your skimmer lower."

Savage shoved the straw hat further down on his brow and opened the door.

"Here goes nothing."

And we were out the door, walking down the little tiled hallway about as casually as two priests in a strip joint. Another flock of tourists paraded down the main corridor and their guide pointed us out. She was a black-haired beauty with hourglass curves.

"On your right you can see two members . . . of the Hits

and Misses?" She had wavered a bit toward the end of the sentence.

I beamed. "That's right."

Excited squeals burst forth from the group and a few ladies broke ranks to press forward with their autograph books. The guide flashed a perfect smile and shrugged helplessly.

I signed a few books "Vance LePantz" and Savage scribbled God knows what. We thanked everybody profusely and headed for the stairs.

"They use the stairs?" I heard a sharp-eyed woman ask the guide. I turned and smiled again. The guide looked at me a little funny, knowing something was out of whack somehow. I blew her a kiss. She pursed her lips, then her face relaxed and she laughed and turned to lead her group. She could have led me anywhere. I followed her progress for just a moment; the wistful shamus remembering a girl who looked like her, a long time before.

We started up the stairs and Savage asked a very germane question.

"LeVine, how many people are in this fool singing group?"

I thought it over. "You mean if it's a lot we get lost in the shuffle and if it's a quartet we're sitting ducks?"

"Exactly."

"We'll just have to see, Mr. Savage. I don't have the slightest idea. Let's just get to 6D, grab some sheet music and sit in a corner for a while."

"Kind of hide?"

"Kind of."

We cautiously opened the door on twenty-six and looked down the hall. It was empty and we ventured out, resplendent in our candy-stripes. My feet were killing me: when I stared down at my shoes I saw them bulging out on the sides.

It was then that Eli W. Savage began humming "Moonlight in Vermont." Loudly. I looked up in amazement and saw two of the heavies coming down the hall toward us.

"You're doing it in D," I told the banker.

"Marty said D."

They were ten feet away, a couple of warehouses with crewcuts.

"Also it's '*pen*-nies in a stream.' Like two words."

They passed by, cursing to themselves. They didn't know us from the Holland Tunnel.

"A *syc*-amore."

They kept walking and we reached 6D, pushing open two large glass doors.

"Very neat, Savage, very neat indeed."

"This detective work is excellent mental exercise." He smiled and shook his head. "Amazingly so."

"Try doing it for a month. You'll *feel* your brain shrinking."

I was conscious of eyes upon us. When I turned around, I noticed that people were already in the audience, gawking at the preparations and studied casualness of the men behind the microphones. Some of the hayseeds were staring at Savage and me. There was a little applause.

The applause continued as we walked to the front of the studio. A wavy-haired guy stepped up to the microphone and pointed to us: "Two of the wonderful Hits and Misses, ladies and gentlemen."

"Bow," I whispered to the banker. We took little half-bows, very relieved. It was clear that there were a lot of Hits and Misses. A young trumpet player winked at me.

"It's those stupid goddamn outfits gets the applause," he said.

Savage and I laughed, uproariously. We were all one big family on "The Pepsodent Show."

The banker and I continued on toward the far side of the studio, passing an accordion player who was rehearsing

"Humoresque." When we saw two more Hits and Misses coming toward us, we veered toward the back of the stage, behind the curtain and out of view of the audience.

Along the right backstage wall, which ran parallel to the corridor past the "L" turn, was a row of windows that faced on the rear of various smaller studios. In 61, I could see Carl Van Doren reading his "World at War" broadcast into a large microphone. Van Doren was alone, yet his emphatic gestures were those of the classroom. 6H was next door. It contained a nervous black-haired man who sat drumming his fingers on the green, felt-covered table. On the table were a mike, a pitcher of water, and two glasses.

I pulled Savage close to me and pointed to the window.

"That's 6H. Who's the guy with the shakes?"

Savage squinted. "That's Feigenbaum."

"I'm sure he'd like to know why all that muscle is hanging out in front of 6H."

"Can't he call the police?"

"And see this place wrecked? There's a million bucks worth of equipment lying around and these boys aren't the kind who just throw their hands in the air when they see a badge. Plus, I'm sure they told him they'd be gone by ten."

Savage kept looking.

"I don't see how we can enter from the rear."

"We can't."

"Then how the hell do we . . ."

I wasn't crazy about the answer, but it was the only one I knew.

"We go in through the front, Mr. Savage. Right under their noses."

I walked over to get a better look into 6H. Three face-sitters were leaning on the wall in the corridor. Two of them were yawning. They'd been promised some action and all they were getting was the wait. Feigenbaum stood up, unlocked a side door and walked into an adjoining studio, 6G. Then he paced back into 6H.

It was ten to ten.

I walked over to Savage.

"How much do you have in your wallet?"

"Oh . . . three hundred."

"Peel off a hundred and give it to me."

"What for?"

"We're going to need a musician to bring this off. I have to pay him something."

"To do what?"

"Just hang on."

I walked back in front of the curtain and climbed into the bandstand, moving toward the friendly trumpet player. He smiled when he saw me, but the closer I got, the more uncertain his smile became. From five feet away, it stopped being a smile altogether.

"You're not with the Hits," he said very loudly.

I hushed him, pulled out my building inspector's shield and announced that I was from the FBI.

"FBI?" He licked his lips nervously.

"Here's a C-note, in return for a small favor." I stuffed the bill into the breast pocket of his green blazer.

"What is this?"

"You want the dough or not? I'll ask someone else."

"No, no," he said urgently. "I'd just like to know."

I wagged a finger at him and started off the bandstand.

"Bring the trumpet."

He followed me backstage, wiping his neck with a handkerchief.

"Where'd you get the outfits?"

I turned on him. "No questions or we forget about the whole deal."

His mouth twitched. Maybe he wasn't going to turn out so hot, but it was getting late.

"What deal?"

"All I want from you is to walk us to Studio 6G like we were all going over a number for the show tonight."

"Who's us?"

I waved Savage over and introduced him as District Supervisor Frank Grimes. He did his part, which was to shut up.

"What are you guys playing tonight?"

" 'Alexander's Ragtime Band.' "

"Terrific. We'll go out the studio door and walk down the corridor. You blow a few notes, explain something, Frank and I will sing or hum, you blow another note. Like that."

"Just that for a hundred bucks?"

I threw him a look and he picked it up for all it was worth.

"There going to be trouble?"

"Not if we do it right. You stay along the inside wall and we'll face you. Remember that. Our heads have to be turned toward you."

The trumpeter mopped his brow. He was kind of a stocky guy, with a plastered hairdo and a thin mustache.

"A hundred bucks is a lotta kale."

" Sure is. You're lucky you smiled at me. Let's shove."

24

THE TRUMPETER WENT OUT FIRST, wandering absently into the middle of the hallway after we had briskly walked along the left side of the studio, drawing admiring glances from the audience. They were being warmed up by the wavy-haired guy.

"Now if anyone has to go to the powder room during the show . . ."

We closed the big glass doors and suddenly it was very quiet. The trumpeter stood in the corridor, nervously fingering his instrument.

"6G," he whispered.

"Check. Left side."

He got close to the wall and started walking.

"Play a couple of notes," I whispered. "And *talk*, goddamit. A hundred smackers, I want talk."

He doodled out the opening bars of "Alexander's." Ta-ta, ta-*ta*, ta-ta, ta-*ta*.

"That where we come in?"

We turned the corner.

"*Talk*," I whispered as roughly as I could. Every pore on my body started dripping.

The trumpeter cleared his throat.

"You guys come in after the first two choruses."

"So it's two choruses of vamp."

"I thought three," said Savage.

We were looking at the trumpeter, our heads screwed stiffly to the left. The trumpeter started stammering and I prayed he wouldn't freeze up solid. From a corner of my eye, I saw the three men leaning against the wall outside 6H. One of them broke away and started down the hall.

"This is bullshit," I heard him mumble to the others.

"Now in the third chorus," the trumpeter finally managed to get out, "Marty says . . ."

Twenty feet from 6G.

"Marty says you guys keep doing 'dip-doo-*ahhh*.'"

Fifteen feet. The thug who thought it was all bullshit passed us, picking his teeth.

"That's it," said Savage. "Doo-*ahhh*."

"No, he's right," I said. "It's 'best band in the land—wah.' A real short wah."

Five feet.

"That's it," said the trumpeter through a veil of perspiration. "Wah." He was nearly paralyzed at the sight of the two truck-sized gents inspecting their nails across from 6H.

We reached 6G.

"Let's go in here and run through it once more." I said it as casually as I could, but it wasn't good enough. I felt I had aroused a good measure of attention.

I tried the knob.

It was locked.

"Locked," I said cheerily. Savage looked ready to faint. I knocked on the door. "Just like these bastards to lock up."

I felt the scrutiny of the two mugs burning a hole through my neck. Then they talked. That was even worse.

"Who are those mugs?"

"Singers."

"Singers? Oldest fuckin' singers . . ."

Feigenbaum came through the adjoining door just as the gorilla made some connections from the gray hair that stuck out beneath Savage's skimmer. I felt for my Colt. Feigenbaum stared at us through the glass and Savage frantically pointed at himself. Feigenbaum's eyes opened wide enough to swim through and he unlocked the door.

"WATCH OUT!"

When the radio exec bellowed, I pulled my gun, turned and fired without even looking. One thug fell immediately, the other grabbed at his wrist. I stepped forward and sapped him very hard. He fell and I knelt down to remove his guns.

Two men turned the corner. I hit one in the kneecap and the other in the shoulder. They hobbled and grabbed at themselves.

I ran into 6C. Feigenbaum locked the door.

"What is this? What's going on?"

I asked him if the glass was bullet-proof.

"It's triple-thick. I can assure you of your safety."

The two thugs started pounding on the door.

"Do they know that?"

"They asked before. I told them." Feigenbaum turned to Savage, who sat slumped in a chair. "You all right, Eli?"

"Some water. Just some water."

"I got to get back to the show," said the trumpeter.

"You'll be a little late. You can't leave here."

He started shaking like a leafless tree in January, the whole business hitting him at once.

"Christ. Christ."

It was five to ten.

"Why don't you gentlemen come into 6H?" Feigenbaum led us into the adjoining studio, just as the two wounded warriors outside attempted to break the windows in with folding chairs. It made kind of a "thunk," like wood hitting wood.

"Eli, sit behind the microphone," said Feigenbaum. He stared at me. "You folks going to use the air time after all? We can cut into the first five minutes of Pepsodent." He paused. "Of course, I'll charge full rates."

The men outside kept trying with the chair until five Pinkertons came on the scene and started wrestling with them.

"You call the Pinks?" I asked.

The radio exec nodded. "I told them to stay close when those gentlemen started hanging around. But they threatened to wreck the equipment if I called for help, so I told the Pinks to stay out of sight. They were down in 5M."

It was three minutes to ten.

"Incredible," Savage said quietly.

"Eli, you ought to give a speech after what I've seen here tonight," Feigenbaum told him. "If this thing has anything to do with the campaign . . ."

"I can't, Herb."

Feigenbaum turned to me.

"Who are those men?"

"Beats me."

His mouth went sour. "It's like that, huh?"

"It's just like that."

He sighed. "I suppose I understand. Never seen anything like it, though, and I've been here a long time." He adjusted his tie. "You're LeVine? The dick?"

"That's right."

Feigenbaum thought that over. "Eli, you going on the air?"

Savage was finally starting to crack. He sat in back of the microphone in his candy-stripes, looking like an aging stud who had just been stood up on New Year's Eve.

"I just can't, Herb." He was almost inaudible. "We're not getting them back, LeVine."

All I could do was shrug. "It's not possible."

The Pinkertons had knocked the two men senseless, after a lot of sweat, and were standing in the hall with their pistols drawn. From the looks of it, they hadn't been drawn since the Boston Police Strike. Suddenly the Pinks were very alert and started shouting at someone down the hall. Inside the studio I heard nothing.

One minute to ten.

Feigenbaum was getting frantic.

"You going on, or not?" He picked up the phone. Savage just sat there shaking his head. He was miserable.

But not nearly as miserable as the little man talking to the Pinkertons.

Not nearly as miserable as Lee Factor.

It was minus forty-five seconds when Factor came into view, carrying a large film case.

"Look like you're about to make a speech," I snapped at Savage.

The banker gawked. "Lee Factor!" The color returned to his cheeks. He whipped off his jacket, undid the bow tie and leaned toward the mike. He looked very good. In fact he thought he was going to make a speech.

"I'm going on, Jack. The hell with it. We'll wreck them."

Factor started beating on the glass. The Pinks tried to restrain him.

"You're going on now or not?" wailed Feigenbaum, waving the telephone receiver.

"Yes, I want to," insisted the banker.

"No!" I yelled at Feigenbaum. "Under no circumstances."

"Jack, I must! I want to!"

"You want Anne to become a national dirty-joke? Are you completely nuts?"

Minus twenty seconds.

"What? What?" Feigenbaum was asking the wall.

"NO, NO, NO!" I bellowed, waving my arms.

"Jack," Savage said desperately. "*Lee Factor*. We can sew this election up. He's standing right here, FDR's boy. It's all ours now."

"He's got the films, you schmuck." I ran to the door and pulled Factor away from the Pinks. He was a trembling puppy of a man. Tears welled in his eyes.

"In here?" I knelt by the film case.

He nodded blankly.

I opened the case and pulled out a reel of film. I unspooled a few feet and held the film up to the light.

Ten o'clock.

And so it was the witching hour of ten when I beheld the loveliest, fullest breasts ever to adorn a banker's daughter. Anne Savage daintily removed her panties and wriggled her hips. She lay down on a bed.

I cleared my throat.

"It's Anne," I told Savage.

"Don't show it to me. Destroy the reel."

I turned to the presidential aide.

"The negative. Give."

He stared at me for a long moment and shook his head heavily, like a horse. Factor's mind wasn't working at all now. It was coming loose in bits and pieces, like branches caught in a swiftly moving stream.

I knelt down again, as "The Pepsodent Show" started coming in through the speakers.

"Ladies and gentlemen, it's 'The *Pep*-sodent Show.'"

"Please," said the trumpeter, who had been sitting quietly. "I got to get back."

"Sure," I said. "Thanks a million."

He got up and slowly went out the door, his trumpet dangling from his left hand. He hadn't the foggiest notion of what he had done or who was involved or why he had done it. All he had was a hundred bucks and enough raw material for a year of nightmares.

I looked through the case.

"No negative here, Factor."

I straightened up and stood inches from Factor. He looked at me and moved his lips. A bubble of saliva formed at his mouth.

"Turn around," I told him. He didn't, so I walked in back of him for a frisk. The negative was in a hidden raincoat pocket. I removed it and held it up.

Factor passed out.

TEN DAYS LATER, Eli and Anne Savage and detective Jack LeVine, of Broadway via Orchard Street, sat around the Savage swimming pool in Aspen, Colorado, clutching highballs and staring out at the Rockies. Kitty Seymour floated lazily in the pool. The sky was as blue as the future.

"Mr. LeVine," said Anne, "I still don't understand why *I* was blackmailed."

"You weren't supposed to be. That's where the whole plan got queered. Fenton's job was to shake down your father, but when he got the films his instincts took over and he realized he could do a little business with you on the side. It was a very dumb play. Butler found out and had him killed, then hired me to put me off the track."

"And Rubine?"

"Rubine's the saddest story of all. They could have let him go and he wouldn't have stopped till he reached the North Pole. But he worked with Fenton and knew the whole story, so they iced him just for insurance."

"It is simply unbelievable," said the banker, sipping reflectively at a Tom Collins. "And what news of Factor?"

"Factor suffered a stroke, a bad one. He'll probably live, if that's what you want to call it. In a few years he should be able to make ashtrays."

Kitty called to me from the pool.

"Jack, the water is delicious. Stop the shop-talk and come in."

"In a second."

"You know Tom and I were talking about you last night, LeVine," said Savage. "About the skill and personal courage you showed throughout this whole affair. He suggested you come on over and join our side."

"Side?"

"The campaign. Help us out with logistical problems. Plus you have a common touch that would help us immeasurably."

"Be the house prole, you mean. Translate what the dumbbell on the street means when he moves his mouth."

"LeVine, you're being extreme." Savage finished his drink with a swallow.

"Father thinks the world of you," said Anne. She lay across an air mattress, wearing a bathing suit that just barely covered the treasures revealed on celluloid. When I looked at her too long, I had trouble with my trunks.

Savage continued his pitch. "LeVine, hasn't this episode revealed to you the moral bankruptcy of the Democratic party?"

"I knew it all along. Listen, Mr. Savage, I'm strictly for LeVine. For your sake, I hope Dewey wins. For my sake I don't care. Let's leave it that way."

"If you say so."

"It's the only way that works."

I got up and took a couple of steps toward the pool. I stuck in my toe.

"Play with me," said Kitty. Her hair streamed water and the drops gleamed in the sun like a crown.

I stepped back, then ran forward and took a long, cool dive, deep into the blue-green water. Down. Down. Away from the noise and the guns and the cheap hotels.

THE PERENNIAL LIBRARY MYSTERY SERIES

Delano Ames

CORPSE DIPLOMATIQUE	P 637, $2.84
FOR OLD CRIME'S SAKE	P 629, $2.84
MURDER, MAESTRO, PLEASE	P 630, $2.84
SHE SHALL HAVE MURDER	P 638, $2.84

E. C. Bentley

TRENT'S LAST CASE	P 440, $2.50
TRENT'S OWN CASE	P 516, $2.25

Gavin Black

A DRAGON FOR CHRISTMAS	P 473, $1.95
THE EYES AROUND ME	P 485, $1.95
YOU WANT TO DIE, JOHNNY?	P 472, $1.95

Nicholas Blake

THE CORPSE IN THE SNOWMAN	P 427, $1.95
THE DREADFUL HOLLOW	P 493, $1.95
END OF CHAPTER	P 397, $1.95
HEAD OF A TRAVELER	P 398, $2.25
MINUTE FOR MURDER	P 419, $1.95
THE MORNING AFTER DEATH	P 520, $1.95
A PENKNIFE IN MY HEART	P 521, $2.25
THE PRIVATE WOUND	P 531, $2.25
A QUESTION OF PROOF	P 494, $1.95
THE SAD VARIETY	P 495, $2.25
THERE'S TROUBLE BREWING	P 569, $3.37
THOU SHELL OF DEATH	P 428, $1.95
THE WIDOW'S CRUISE	P 399, $2.25
THE WORM OF DEATH	P 400, $2.25

Andrew Garve

THE ASHES OF LODA	P 430, $1.50
THE CUCKOO LINE AFFAIR	P 451, $1.95
A HERO FOR LEANDA	P 429, $1.50
MURDER THROUGH THE LOOKING GLASS	P 449, $1.95
NO TEARS FOR HILDA	P 441, $1.95
THE RIDDLE OF SAMSON	P 450, $1.95

Michael Gilbert

BLOOD AND JUDGMENT	P 446, $1.95
THE BODY OF A GIRL	P 459, $1.95
THE DANGER WITHIN	P 448, $1.95
FEAR TO TREAD	P 458, $1.95

Joe Gores

HAMMETT	P 631, $2.84

C. W. Grafton

BEYOND A REASONABLE DOUBT	P 519, $1.95
THE RAT BEGAN TO GNAW THE ROPE	P 639, $2.84

Edward Grierson

THE SECOND MAN	P 528, $2.25

Bruce Hamilton

TOO MUCH OF WATER	P 635, $2.84

If you enjoyed this book you'll want to know about
THE PERENNIAL LIBRARY MYSTERY SERIES
Buy them at your local bookstore or use this coupon for ordering:

Qty	P number	Price
_____	_____	_____
_____	_____	_____
_____	_____	_____
_____	_____	_____
_____	_____	_____
_____	_____	_____
_____	_____	_____
_____	_____	_____
_____	_____	_____
_____	_____	_____
_____	_____	_____
_____	_____	_____
_____	_____	_____

	postage and handling charge	$1.00
	_____ book(s) @ $0.25	_____
	TOTAL	[ ]

Prices contained in this coupon are Harper & Row invoice prices only.
They are subject to change without notice, and in no way reflect the prices at
which these books may be sold by other suppliers.

**HARPER & ROW, Mail Order Dept. #PMS, 10 East 53rd St., New
York, N.Y. 10022.**
Please send me the books I have checked above. I am enclosing $_____
which includes a postage and handling charge of $1.00 for the first book and
25¢ for each additional book. Send check or money order. No cash or
C.O.D.s please

Name_____

Address_____

City_____ State_____ Zip_____
Please allow 4 weeks for delivery. USA only. This offer expires 9/30/84.
Please add applicable sales tax.